TOO LATE
TO RUN

JUDY SNIDER

World Castle Publishing, LLC
Pensacola, Florida
Copyright © Judy Snider
Paperback ISBN: 9781629894898
eBook ISBN: 9781629894904
First Edition World Castle Publishing, LLC, July 18, 2016
http://www.worldcastlepublishing.com

Licensing Notes
Cover: Karen Fuller
Editor: Maxine Bringenberg

CHAPTER 1

Maggie always woke up at five, which annoyed her. When she was a teenager she could sleep in, but those days were gone. Actually they were gone once her first son was born. Every cough, every sigh, from then on she heard everything. Now she automatically woke up, and once awake she was doomed to stay awake. It also didn't help that her cat, Bailey, nibbled on her hair and kissed her face to be fed every morning.

But this morning had been special. Her sister from Michigan was coming to visit her in Virginia, then they would go on their week long dream trip to a wooded island resort about an hour away. She wanted to make sure she had all her favorite foods in the house for her visit. She had jumped out of bed, fed Bailey, and showered quickly. She still liked to have candy by her sister's bedside and clean sheets on the bed, but she would do that when she got back from the store.

Maggie thought back to that morning and how it started out not much different than her other mornings...yet there was that feeling that she could not put her finger on, the feeling of a cloud over her that she dismissed as just not enough sleep, the cat meowing for food, or her dreams that came and went since her husband's death. If Maggie had not been so impatient to go to the store so early in the morning, the nightmare she was in might never have happened.

The grocery store was only about ten minutes away, so she threw on her usual jeans and sweater and headed out the door. There were lots of cars out for a Saturday morning, so Maggie decided to avoid the busy roads and take the shortcut she had found.

When she made that turn onto Eclipse Lane, she felt a random feeling of unease. There were no houses in this section, but mostly flat-roofed wooden businesses that sat side by side. The businesses looked dark and the parking lots empty this early in the morning. As she drove by the last business she noticed the front of a white car by the back of it, and saw a dim light on in the store's front window. *Odd*, Maggie thought, because she saw the car had no plates. Maggie had a habit of checking out everyone's plates quickly to see if they were from a different state. She had done this since she was a little kid, and her parents used to make time go faster on long car trips by having Maggie and her two sisters look at license plates.

Maggie had just passed the white car when a loud popping sound come from her car, and she lost control of it as pieces of her right tire flew into the air. She knew not to slam on the brakes, but her heart was racing as she let the car glide into one of the parking lots.

Oh no, feeling shaky, not today, not here. She sat still, her hands holding the steering wheel in a death grip, trying to think what to do next. Her first thought was that she would not get everything done for her sister's arrival in the afternoon. But then she wondered how she was going to change the tire.

"I know, I know," Maggie said to herself. "I'm an independent woman, I should be able to change a tire." But she had always counted on Henry to do those things. She thought of calling her automobile company, but in her rush to get out of the house she had left her cell phone in her other sweater pocket. Now she was beginning to get nervous…flat tire, no cell phone, back road.

Not a very smart girl, Maggie, she scolded herself. Suddenly it dawned on her that the business was open a short walk back, by the white car, and they could help her. A sense of relief washed over her and she grabbed her purse and started walking. No cars were coming down the street, but she picked up her pace, thankful that it was not nighttime.

She did not know what made her suddenly step off the road and stop walking, as if someone had whispered in her ear, "Don't go any further."

Just then the door of the business opened and a man came out and jumped into the white car. He did not see her, but screeched the car out of the lot. *Oh no*, Maggie groaned, *now where am I going to make a call from*? She felt her heart start to speed up again, and the next second there was a loud explosion, and an enormous wave of hot air hit Maggie's face. The sound, heat, and flames were the last thing Maggie remembered before her body fell backwards like a rag doll and hit the ground hard, falling into darkness.

***

Maggie heard a faint voice calling her name. "Mrs. Andrews, Mrs. Andrews." Maggie could feel the pain in her head that screamed at her, blocking out the sound of the person's voice telling her, "You're okay, Mrs. Andrews, open

7

your eyes slowly. I'm checking your vision, so you will see a bright light."

She felt the softness under her as if she was still lying in bed. She slowly opened her eyes and saw the glare of a flashlight in her eyes, and smelled the pungent smell of burning wood in her nostrils.

"My name is Sandy. I'm a volunteer paramedic with the city of Moline. You have been hurt. We are going to get you to the hospital." After seeing Maggie's hand fly up to the hard collar around her neck, the paramedic reassured her. "You have a brace around your neck. It's routine procedure. Do you know where you are? Do you know what day this is?" Sandy asked gently. "Are you in any pain?"

Maggie said groggily, "This is Saturday, I was walking, and my head is killing me."

Maggie knew what day it was. She remembered her sister was coming, and she remembered the explosion…she could not remember much else. Suddenly her sister's face came to mind, and she thought, *Oh, no.* She mumbled something about her wallet and her sister's number in it.

Sandy said they were taking her to Vine Hospital, which was about five minutes from Maggie's house.

"Please lie back and we will get you fixed up in no time. Don't worry about your sister and family. Your information was in your purse we found by you. They will be called, I promise."

It suddenly sank in…an explosion. *What on earth happened?* She began to shake uncontrollably. *Oh, my God, am I going to be paralyzed? How bad am I hurt?* she screamed to herself as she sank more and more into panic. She had always been calm to the world, but her real self, who could get anxious in a second flat, was here in full force. Seeing the blood and cuts on her hand did not help her feelings of helplessness.

As they secured her with safety belts and lifted her into the truck, she could not see down the road due to the neck brace, she could only look up. She heard someone say, "Oh, no. Here come the media. Let's get her out of here quickly. She is not up to answering any questions."

Now as she looked at the building from the safety of the ambulance, she felt her stomach turn as she saw the shell of what used to be the business, burned to a crisp.

CHAPTER 2

That was the last voice she heard before her eyes started to close. As she started to fade out, exhausted, she heard them say, "No more offices, just firefighters and flames. Boy, is she lucky that she was down the road, or it would have been a whole other story."

Maggie was wheeled into the hospital emergency room swaddled like a baby to keep her from moving, and quickly put into one of the back exam rooms. A young woman with a stethoscope around her neck and a white coat stood looking at a laptop computer on a cart. Maggie had been a social worker in a hospital as one of her jobs in life, so it did not surprise her to see someone trying to see what was going on.

"Hi," Maggie said wearily.

The doctor looked up from the screen and smiled at Maggie broadly. "Hello, I'm Doctor Mills, a neurosurgeon, and we will be running a number of tests today to make sure you're okay. I'm going to start with a neurological exam, and then we will do a CT scan. I promise I will keep you posted along the way. I will have the nurse come in to clean up those cuts and scrapes for you. We will try to get you up to a room as soon as possible. I can say, after what just happened, you're one lucky lady."

Dr. Mills was very kind and considerate to Maggie as she gave her a very thorough exam. Social worker or not, she was scared out of her wits about this, and Dr. Mills's kind manner helped to calm her down. She was worried she would have severe damage to her neck or spine. Dr. Mills assured her that the neurological exam proved negative, but Maggie wanted to see the CT scan results as well. After the CT scan was completed they took Maggie to her room and started an IV of fluids to hydrate and relax her, and she slipped off into the deepest sleep she had had in a long time.

***

"This is Reggie Page from Channel 21 News reporting from Moline. Our top story today is the explosion on Eclipse Street early this morning. Firefighters were able to put out the blaze after a few hours, but the explosion is under investigation. There was no one inside the business at the time, but a woman standing nearby was injured. We do not have any details at this time regarding why she was there or if she had a connection to the blaze. Watch our Five O'clock News for the latest update. This is Reggie Page, reporting from Channel 21 News."

Reggie thought, *Thank goodness I'm done for the day. I love this job, but this summer heat at times is just unbearable.* Of course, covering an explosion and fire did not help. Reggie was ready to go home and take a shower, then meet friends later at their favorite Thai restaurant. Tomorrow her employer would have her camping out in front of the hospital trying to get a scoop on Mrs. Andrews from her relatives or doctors regarding her condition. Reggie knew she should probably head over to the hospital now, having missed the woman before she was taken away. She also expected a call from her station manager, but since she had been on a five day work schedule with little sleep, her usual eagerness to cover a story was gone.

Reggie was twenty-eight and lived alone. She was from Boston, and had held her position at the station for one year. She was the rookie who, rain or shine, would be out getting a story. Her parents kept suggesting she get a roommate or live in a safer area, but Reggie would just look at them and say, "Do you know how many murders and robberies I cover? I'm very careful, so you don't have to worry about me. Maybe I'll get a guard dog," she'd joked. Her parents were not amused. They only wanted to make sure she was safe and secure in her apartment. Reggie always said, "Don't worry, Mom." and her mom would hug her and say, "I will stop worrying about you when I die, and until then, no matter how old you are, I will worry." After every visit, her parents would say, "We love you, be careful."

"Hey, Reggie," Joe, her cameraman, called to her. "Want to head over to the hospital?"

"Not today, Joe," she said. "How about if you pick me up early tomorrow and we will try for the story then, if that's okay with Bill?"

Joe said, "I'll text him now and see what he says. No sense in heading out if he wants us there now."

Reggie watched Joe send the text and then listened as Joe read Bill's return text, and frowned. "Guess your idea won't cut it with Bill. He wants us over there now to make sure this gets on the Five O'clock News *today*."

"Damn it," Reggie muttered to Joe. "Okay, okay, whatever Bill wants, but at least let me stop and grab a sandwich and soda to go. I'm starved."

Reggie jumped back into the station van and checked her not so perfect dark brown hair and her starting-to-melt-from-the-heat makeup on her light Mediterranean skin. She would have to do a quick fix up before being on air again.

***

Little did she know that someone in her very own city had been watching her coverage of the story, and was eager to learn just as much as Reggie did about this woman who they said may have been a witness…yes, very eager, and very furious.

CHAPTER 3

Maggie woke up with a hand holding hers. She looked up to see her sister, Alice, smiling at her softly.

"Well, Maggie, I see that my little sister has been up to more shenanigans again," she laughed. Maggie could tell she was trying to lighten the mood with her humor. "I spoke with your neurosurgeon and I was told you are going to be fine. You have a concussion from your fall, and they need to watch you for a while and wake you every hour for twenty-four hours. You are going to hurt like hell for a while, but you are lucky you weren't hurt worse than you were. Maggie, I'm worried about how frightening this has been for you. I'm so glad I'm here visiting with you. The police came in to talk to you, but you were out of it, so they will come back. For now, I won't ask you what happened."

"No, Alice," Maggie looked at her eyes. "I want to tell you about it. Some of it I can't remember, and I'm tired, but please just sit and listen."

"For a few minutes, but if I see you becoming worn out or upset, I want you to stop. Is it a deal?"

"It's a deal. Well, you know how I like to go to the store early. Today, since you were coming for a visit, I started out much earlier, and decided to take a shortcut to get to the store. On the way I had a blowout. I forgot my cell phone at home so I started walking toward a business I saw that I thought may have a telephone I could use. As I was walking towards it, the building blew up, and I flew backwards." Maggie knew by the look on her sister's face what she was thinking. "Alice, this is not because I went to the store for you. There must have been a gas explosion. Thank goodness the person in the white car got out."

"What white car, Maggie?"

Just as Maggie was about to answer, two policemen walked into her room.

"Mrs. Andrews, do you mind if we speak with you?" the older policeman with grey hair and a beard said to her. "We won't take up much of your time. I'm Detective Adams, and this is Detective Mike Pierce."

"Yes, as long as my sister can stay in the room with me, that would be fine." Maggie did not trust herself to speak clearly or remember much after the fire.

"Absolutely," Detective Pierce said.

"I was just telling Alice that I went to the store early, took a shortcut, and had a blowout. I then walked towards a business I saw to use their phone since I forgot my cell phone at home. Just as I got close to the business, I heard this loud explosion and saw flames coming from the building. The next thing I remember I woke up and the paramedics were there." Maggie was surprised how many of the details she remembered, since she was suffering from a concussion.

"Did you know anyone at this business?"

"No, I was just on my way to the store," Maggie said, a little confused as to why they might think she knew anyone at that business.

"Are you sure?"

"Yes, I'm sure; I was headed to the store, and thought I could use their phone. I don't even remember the names of any businesses there."

"Why would you think you could use the phone there at that time of the morning, since those businesses are closed?"

"I saw a light on inside one of the offices, and the front end of a white car when I first drove by, and then I saw it leave just as I was coming back and getting close to the building. As the building exploded, I remember thinking, 'Oh, no, there goes my phone call.'"

"Could you tell who was driving the white car that you saw?"

"No," Maggie said, now feeling a little light headed. "I saw a man come out, but I was not that close that I could see his face."

"Can you give us any type of description of this man?"

"I can't. I do know he was white, not tall or short…dark wavy hair."

"Was there anyone else in the car?"

"I don't know. I was only looking at the front of the car," Maggie said wrinkling her brow trying to remember, and feeling pain from doing that.

"Did you see the license plate number?"

Now Maggie was starting to get annoyed. She wanted to say, "What the hell, I'm in the hospital with a concussion, I almost died, and you want to know if I saw the license plate number?"

"No, I don't remember even seeing the license plate."

"But you did see the driver."

Alice interrupted. "I think she has answered all the questions she can for now. She has a concussion, and you gentlemen know you can't remember much with a concussion. It's a serious brain injury. Could you please come back later?"

Detective Pierce looked a little annoyed, and looked like he was about to say something else when he changed his mind and said, "Sorry, you've been through a lot. We have additional questions for you, but we will come back. If you remember anything, you call me. If not, we'll be back tomorrow." He laid his card on the tray table by the side of her bed. "Nice meeting you both."

***

Detective Pierce was at the end of the hall before he turned to Detective Adams and looked back towards Maggie's room. "I know, I know, you're going to ask me if I think something is funny about her story. She seems like a nice lady. Hard to imagine that she could be involved in a bombing, if it was a bomb, but we've seen stranger cases than this before. I want to talk to her tomorrow, here or at her home, depending on when they discharge her. Let's head back to the precinct and see if any more information has been gathered."

Usually Detective Pierce and his partner would handle most of the initial investigation, but with a bombing there were a lot of other departments involved. Depending on the circumstances of the situation, whether hurting one person or taking out a business, Homeland Security or the FBI may also be involved. It was too early to tell the scope of it all. The bomb squad was at the scene along with the firefighters. Moline's sheriff had already called in the Evidence Recovery Team, and Pierce would make the call to the FBI also. It was being investigated to see what types of businesses were located in the strip of buildings that were affected. Could be as simple as someone who owned the business, and after leaving, a gas leak was the cause, whether by accident or for insurance fraud. It was believed that five businesses in a row were blown up, so all owners needed to be contacted. At the moment it was not known if all had alarm systems or surveillance cameras.

Mike Pierce liked this part of his job. He had become a detective to follow in his uncle's footsteps, but he liked the mysteries that he had to solve. He did not like to have people die or be seriously hurt, and was glad this fire had killed no one. Mike's wife, Annie, used to say he loved his job more than her, and he would grab her, wrap her in his arms, and say, "You're right, Annie Monroe." He would then give her a long passionate kiss, smelling her Shalimar perfume on her neck, looking into her crystal blue eyes, and telling her that he loved her a lot. Annie would laugh and snuggle in close. He knew that she hid, as best as she could, her fear that she would get a call that he was dead. Little did either of them know that it would be Annie who would pass away first from an aneurysm, and Mike the one who would get the call that she had died suddenly. All he remembered was crying like a wounded animal and yelling into the phone, "Is this some kind of joke?" His heart had never been the same, and the feeling that he should have known something was wrong haunted him still.

Mike's partner asked him a question, and he snapped back from that horrible memory of five years ago to the present. "What was your question? Sorry, I spaced out for a moment. Must be a senior moment," he laughed, glad for the interruption of his thoughts of Annie.

"How about we take another run over to the fire before

we head back? The station can send us any information via our phones if we need it right away."

"That sounds good to me. You and I could maybe use our sixth senses and vision to find out anything new."

Mike headed towards the coffee cart as he said to Detective Stephens, "I think Mrs. Andrews knows more than she is telling us. Maybe tomorrow she will remember more.

"It would be horrible if we find out she set the bomb."

**

As they came out of the front of the hospital they did not notice the person standing over to the side of the bench looking at a map, yet glancing up to look at them.

A little way from Mike and his partner, the man with the map heard what they said and smiled. "Yes, wouldn't it be horrible if we find out she set the bomb…so very horrible."

CHAPTER 4

Reggie got out of the news van a block from the hospital. She wanted to try to find out more information about Maggie Andrews. They would not let her in the hospital with the cameras, and if they saw the Channel 21 News van security would be called. She hated in some ways to snoop where people were sick. With all the HIPAA patient privacy laws, she could not even ask if the lady was in the hospital or what room she was in.

Reggie darted into the hospital and went into the ladies' room by the cafeteria. She stood at the mirror combing her hair until someone came into the restroom.

While they were washing their hands, Reggie said, "Wow, can you believe all the commotion here? It must be that explosion victim brought in this morning."

The woman looked directly at her now and got very animated as she said, "Oh yes, that has been the buzz of the hospital. She is on the same floor as my father, so we saw when she came to the floor. I feel bad for her. When I go home I want to watch the news and find out more, but my dad gets upset easily so the TV has been turned off."

Reggie breathed a sigh of relief that this woman did not know who she was. "So, is the entire fifth floor covered with police?"

"Oh, she's not on the fifth floor, she is on three like my dad. Do you have a relative in here?"

"Whoops, that must be my phone; nice talking to you," Reggie said quickly, as if her phone vibrated and she felt it. She may be a reporter and always trying to get a story, but to directly lie and say she had a sick relative at the hospital, she just couldn't do it.

Reggie saw the bank of elevators, and as the door opened on one of them, she jumped in quickly and headed up to the third floor. It would be easy to see where the mystery woman was. How many rooms would have a guard outside of them? At least she hoped they didn't. She walked down the hall looking quite confident, and as she came to the end, looked down one of the side halls and spotted a guard sitting outside of a room.

As she hesitated, she saw an attractive woman come out of the room and head towards the vending machines. Reggie had visited many people at this hospital, so she knew the halls like the back of her hand. Reggie followed her to the vending machines and got her money out. Something about this woman told her that she was not one to fall for any lines.

"Hello, I'm Reggie Page of Channel 21 News, and I came up here to interview the woman involved in the explosion. I saw you come out of the room. Are you family?"

***

Maggie's sister was startled, but calmly said, "I don't think this is a good time for you to talk with her, and I think you just showing up is certainly NOT okay. My sister is recovering, and too many visitors are not letting her get any rest." Alice could feel herself getting agitated, and her sisterly protection was starting to show.

"I'm sorry, but I really do want to find out what happened, to see if this was a gas explosion or if someone did this deliberately. I do want to see them caught," Reggie said sincerely.

Alice grabbed her soda from the machine and looked into Reggie's eyes. "Go away. You may be trying to help, but right now you're not."

"Can I ask you a few questions then?" Reggie said, not moving out of Alice's way.

"No." she said, going around Reggie.

"But what if it was a person who did this, and they try to come here?"

Alice spun around and gave Reggie a shocked look. She realized if it was easy for Reggie to find her sister, if there was a bomber, he might find her sister as well. She sighed and said, "Okay, you have two minutes. But do not release what room or floor she's on, or any other information about her. I could only hope the guard does his job and protects her. What do you want to know?" she said, sinking down onto one of the few chairs in the vending room.

"Tell me why she was near the building that blew up."

Alice did not know how much to say and probably the detectives should be here, she thought.

Reggie said, "We know her name is Maggie Andrews and she lives on Farmington Street. I want to know if she knew anyone in the buildings, does she always drive that road, who are you, and why was she on that road so early in the morning?"

"I'm her sister, she did not know anyone at that building, and she was just going out grocery shopping that early when she had a tire blowout."

"A tire blowout," Reggie said with real sympathy. "Oh, your poor sister. Was it in front of that building?"

"Nearby. That's why she was walking towards the building…to ask if she could use their telephone."

"Did she see anyone?"

Alice was starting to get very uncomfortable. If she told this woman about the white car, it could put her sister in danger, but it could also help find out how this happened to her.

"I don't know. My sister has been hurt and has a concussion. She did say that she saw a white car, but who knows exactly what she remembers? I must go now…that is *enough* questions." Alice said with a voice that had turned cold and icy.

"Thanks," Reggie said as Alice started for the door. "I hope your sister gets better soon. Maybe we can talk more when she returns home?"

"Maybe, but for now please leave us alone."

***

Reggie headed down to the van and told her photographer to get ready to do shots in front of the hospital. She would not say what floor Maggie was on or say she had seen a white car, but she would mention that sources told her Maggie was going out shopping, had a blow-out, and was walking towards the building to use their telephone right before the explosion. She certainly could have mentioned the car, but Reggie had a bad feeling in her "reporter" gut. Besides, she was curious as to what that white car had to do with anything, and made up her mind to talk to Maggie herself soon. Reggie had one brother, and she knew not to mention Maggie had a sister at all. It could put her in danger if it was a bombing and intentional, not just some accident.

"Hello, this is Reggie Page reporting to you from Vine Hospital...."

***

Maggie woke up the next day very sore and stiff. She knew exactly where she was and smiled when she saw Alice sitting in a chair by the bed, actually staring at her. She started to move her arm to wave, but the pain made her wave one finger instead.

"Hi, Susan," Maggie said brightly. "Do you think this hotel has room service?"

Alice frowned and was about to say something when Maggie burst out laughing.

"Ha, you thought I was off my rocker, Alice." She laughed until she realized it made her ribs hurt.

"Oh, you," Alice said, gently patting her on her arm. "Injured, and you still have the time to tease me. Really, how are you Maggie?"

"I'm sore and a little groggy, but pretty good. My head hurts like hell, but hey, at least I'm alive. What I really need is coffee. *Please* get me coffee. That is all I need, a caffeine withdrawal headache on top of how I feel...yikes."

"Coffee is coming up, Maggie. The doctor came in and said she would be back." Alice then said, "Thank goodness you gave permission for me to hear about your tests. The doctor said that you could go home in the afternoon sometime since all of your tests look good. Concussion, scrapes, bruises, some ringing in the ears for a while, but no broken bones. Yah, now I don't have to carry you around."

24

"You may, Alice, if I don't get up and walk a little."

Just as Maggie told Alice she needed to get up, a nurse came in and introduced herself and helped Maggie to the bathroom.

Another person came in with a tray and set it down on the table by her bed. "Your sister was in no condition to order breakfast last night, so we have scrambled eggs, a biscuit, sausage, orange juice, and coffee for her now. Her nurse said she did not have any dietary restrictions."

"Thanks." Alice said while she took the top off the coffee and put it aside for her. She straightened the bed a little and put out some clothes she had brought from Maggie's home for her to change into.

When Maggie came out of the bathroom the nurse helped her to her chair to eat. She saw the clothes on the bed, and seemed to shift from a teasing sister to a very somber woman. She did remember being told they would have to bag her clothes for evidence, and she suddenly had a flash of what happened yesterday. She had worked with patients with PTSD, but had never experienced it herself. She suddenly felt a little lightheaded, and started to get very anxious.

Now calm down, Maggie, she told herself. *Try your deep breathing. You are okay, you are not having a heart attack, but you have every right to be anxious. For God's sake, you were in an explosion.* Maggie closed her eyes and started to do her relaxation breathing. Actually, when her husband died she'd had anxiety attacks also, and found her deep breathing helped.

"Are you okay, Maggie?"

"Fine, just realizing how lucky I am and feeling like it all just happened. I will be fine, I just need to relax." She finished her breathing and, feeling better, started to sip her coffee and eat her breakfast.

25

"I'm going to go back to your house and shower, and then I'll come back," Alice said. "See you soon. Love you."

"Love you too," Maggie said softly.

By the time Alice returned Maggie was dressed, had talked to the neurosurgeon, and was cleared to go with an appointment set up in one week. She had instructions on how to clean her abrasions. With Alice there the nurse went over home instructions. She told her who to call if she started to get headaches, felt dizzy, or her vision blurred. They said her tests were fine, but there were things to look for. If she did have any of the symptoms they discussed, they wanted to do a CT scan to make sure there was no bleeding going on in her brain. *It is always good to have that second ear to remember details of medicine, etc.,* Maggie thought, still having moments of fuzziness.

***

Just as they were about to step out the hospital room door, Detective Pierce and his partner entered.

"Hello, Mrs. Andrews, we were hoping we could ask you a few more questions."

Detective Pierce noticed the distress and annoyance on Maggie's face.

"Why not, Detective? But I really want to get out of this place and get in my own bed."

"We won't keep you for long. We still need some details about yesterday. We can come to your house another time if this is too much for you."

"Okay, ask away," Maggie sighed, sitting back down in the high backed chair.

"Can you describe the driver of the car?"

"He was white, with brown hair, and looked to be of average height. But I was a distance away from him when he got into the car. Just as I was going by, I saw a little of the white car, but did not see him then. It was near the end business, and I hoped they would be open so I could use their phone."

"And you said you had never been there?"

"No, I just wanted to get to the store because my sister was coming over."

"And you didn't know anyone at this business?"

Maggie was sensing they were not telling her something. "Do you doubt my story?"

"No, we just need to gather all the facts."

Then he listed all of the businesses there. One of them sounded familiar to Maggie.

"Wait, I have used one of them, but they just came to my house. I didn't even know they were located there. It's a blind company. They did my vertical blinds…when was that?" Maggie's head was starting to hurt at trying to remember, and she said, "I'm not trying to be difficult. I'm just tired, have a concussion, and don't really remember all of the details… please just let me go home for now."

"Sorry, Mrs. Andrews," Mike said, feeling a little sorry for the woman. She looked like a cat that had been in a fight with her face scratched, and there was something about her that made him not want to press more questions. *She is an attractive lady even with all the scratches*, Mike thought. *Stop*, he chastised himself. He usually did not think of any people he interviewed in terms of their appearance, but something about her attracted him.

"We'll be contacting you at home. Hope everything goes well for you," Mike said as he left.

***

Maggie actually believed the detective when he said he hoped all went well, and he seemed nice enough, but she just wanted to leave. As Maggie slowly started to leave with her sister, the ward clerk at the desk said, "Oh, Mrs. Andrews, you take care." She turned to Alice and Maggie and said, "It was nice meeting you both, and also meeting your brother. What a nice man he was."

"Brother? You must be mistaken. We don't have a brother. He must have been here for one of the other patients."

"He said he was going to go down to the room and could find it himself. Maybe I did have the wrong person," the ward clerk said, sounding confused.

He never came in, Maggie thought. *They must meet lots of people on the floor, and this was someone else's brother.*

Yet, as they started to leave the desk, Maggie felt the faintest shiver run through her.

Chapter 5

Mike's shift was over and all he wanted to do was go home to his apartment and swim in the pool.

He liked swimming because he was able to go out in public dressed in regular clothes, instead of a uniform and all the reactions that caused. Some people were friendly when they saw him, some fearful, and some just gave him an icy stare. At the pool he was just like anybody else. Sure, in some ways he was always "on," like in the movies, but he always hoped wherever he went would be quiet, with no drama that he had to intervene in.

It was still lonely without Annie. He dated off and on, and everybody wanted to find the perfect girl for him, but even after five years he had just not wanted anything more than a few dates with any one person. His being somewhat older didn't stop his dating, but not all the girls understood that at his age every once and awhile he got a getting older ache or pain, and he wasn't a young stud. He laughed when he thought of that word, and hadn't ever thought he was a stud. He could have led a few that were interested on, but he had never been raised that way. His mom was a school teacher and his dad did consulting work. They were just two honest, hardworking people.

Besides, having been married to Annie for five years had been the best years of his life, and he couldn't imagine anyone ever being like her. She was funny, witty, and odd at times, but she was his Annie. He had met her at a bar. They were both uncomfortable to be there in some ways, but when he asked her to dance, and they later danced one slow dance, he knew he was smitten by her. It was not just her looks, but her sense of humor was a joy. He had dated a few girls, each for one year, but something was missing. When his first date with Annie was over, he knew in his heart that she was going to be the one he married. They dated for less than a year, but by that time they both knew there was no sense of postponing a wedding. They had not lived together, and were ready just to be in the same place all the time.

He was thinking of her more today because of the woman who was involved in the explosion. There was something about her that stirred up memories of Annie. He didn't know if it was because she had similar looks to Annie or if it was something else, but something had made Mike's heartstrings ache a little more today.

He had major investigating to do tomorrow, but as he drove into his apartment complex he made himself think of cool water, a steak on the grill, a beer, and a good movie to watch tonight on his fifty inch television.

***

Maggie could feel herself relax as her sister helped her out of the car. Home…thank God, she was home. All she wanted

30

to do was laugh with her sister, have Alice throw a steak on the grill for them later, have a beer, and watch a good movie tonight. Well, actually, even one beer she debated on, but the steak and movie sounded good. *Steak cut up in small pieces*, she thought, feeling her sore jaw with her hand.

As she opened the front door, she remembered she had not made it to the store, did not have steaks, or for that matter any of the groceries she had wanted to get in the house for her sister. She turned to Alice. "Damn, Alice, I was going to make you a steak yesterday, but I never made it to the store, and now you'll be lucky if you get a bowl of cereal for dinner."

"Ha! I thought you'd worry about that. I went to the store and brought back some steaks, salad stuff, and beer. If you were on meds, I would not let you have any beer, but you're not on meds. I checked with your doctor, so your wild one beer you have every evening won't hurt, you big lush," Alice smiled.

"Oh, don't start me laughing," Maggie said, holding her ribs and wincing a little. "Ha, ha, my ribs are really sore, but hey, I'm here…could be worse."

Maggie's house was in a cul-de-sac and was the house she and her husband had lived in for years. It was a cozy, light-filled one story, and she had decided just to stay there after her husband's death. Besides, she had Lila, a close friend who lived across the street and did volunteer projects with her. When Maggie's sons came back to see her, they came back to this home and memories of their dad.

They walked into the house and were greeted by Maggie's cat, Bailey. She had had her for years, and Bailey was just starting to get that senior cat boniness.

"Hi, my girl," Maggie said, taking Bailey gently into her arms and rubbing her cheek against Bailey's soft fur.

"Mamma's home, and you get extra treats."

"Please sit down, Maggie," Alice ordered. "You really need to rest, and hey, use me while I'm here to be your servant…no smartass remarks, please. Really, sit down and I'll get everything ready. Just rest, and maybe take a nap. Your body and brain had quite a shock."

"I'm getting a little weary. Maybe I will take a nap. I just want to use the bathroom and wash my face. That is, around the cuts and scrapes. Remind me to put on the antibiotic ointment later please, Alice."

Maggie went into the bathroom with Alice not far behind, worried she could faint. She started to run the water and looked over behind the toilet. The window was open and a hot breeze was coming in. *Funny*, Maggie thought, *I must have been in such a hurry that I forgot I opened the window. I probably opened it after my shower, to get the humidity out.* But Maggie frowned as she tried hard to remember opening it and couldn't. Alice probably opened it, if she didn't.

Maggie was startled to see herself in the mirror, but knew she would heal. She was lucky. Weary, she went to the other room and faded off to a deep sleep, with an image of the open window the last thing she remembered.

***

Reggie did make it home in time to go out with friends. She had always had a nice set of girl friends in life, and this city was no different. She had met Tonya at the station, and Tonya had introduced her to some of her friends. Within a year she had a small group of friends who liked to go to movies, restaurants, and try new things. At twenty-eight she was still looking for her "soul mate" in life, but except for one guy she'd dated for a few years, she had not found her "someone." She actually felt there were probably a lot of people in life she could be happy with, but with her crazy hours and dislike of bars, she had a hard time even finding someone to date. She was going to try one of the online dating services soon...she had two friends who had met their husbands that way. Her friends occasionally tried to fix her up, but her quirky sense of humor sometimes scared guys off. Why couldn't she find a guy who liked a weird sense of humor, was sensitive, could cook, and could stand her being out all times of the day on a story? Her mom always told her not to settle, to be herself, and not to become a chameleon and try to be whatever a guy wanted her to be. Sometimes having parents who had been happily married for thirty years set the bar high for Reggie.

At the Thai restaurant she and her friends did get a drink sent over from a handsome man at the bar, but Reggie knew he must have been looking at her blonde friend, Susan, who turned heads wherever she went. Susan was a lawyer at a nearby firm. Susan thought that Reggie should be proud of her looks, as she was attractive and there was an air of mystery about her. Also, with her being on the news, Susan thought every guy wanted to meet Reggie Page of Channel 21. Reggie would laugh and go into her reporter voice, and her friends would laugh hysterically. They did not care that she was a reporter but loved her zaniness, and she was a true devoted friend. Just as she thought, the handsome guy at the bar slipped a card to Susan and said something softly to her. Susan laughed and put the card in her purse, waving as he walked out of the restaurant.

"It's time for me to go home, girls." Reggie announced.

"See you on the news tomorrow, Reggie. Let us know what happened to that woman over on Eclipse Street."

"Will do," Reggie said as she left with Carol. She had only had one drink, but Carol did not have any so she had said she would be the designated driver.

Carol lived in the same apartment complex as Reggie, and in fact was one floor down from her. She had dirty blonde hair and freckles, and usually wore her hair in a sleek pony tail. She would never tell her true age, but she looked to be in her early thirties. Reggie had looked her up on the computer but could not find out much about her, just her real estate information. She could have done a more intensive search, but she felt she would have been out of line to do that to a friend.

They would get together to go to the pool occasionally or watch a movie, and Carol was very nice. Yet, Reggie always felt that there was something about Carol that she couldn't put her finger on. Aloofness sometimes, something secretive. Carol had broken up with a boyfriend a year ago, about the time Reggie moved in, but did not like to talk about it very much. He was married, and Reggie had never met him. In fact, when Reggie would ask her for details, she would get very quiet and say she had put that in the past and did not want to discuss it, except to say with a very blank face, "What goes around, comes around." Carol was a real estate agent so had strange hours like Reggie, and traveled often too, so tonight they both were eager to go home to their own apartments.

"Thanks for the ride, Carol. I owe you a pizza sometime for all the times you drive me," Reggie said as she headed up the stairs to her apartment.

"No problem, Reggie," Carol said, waving goodnight.

As she climbed the steps she thought she heard Carol say something else in a low voice. "What?"

Carol didn't answer and went into her apartment. *Must have been talking to herself, like I do,* Reggie thought as she shut the door to her apartment and got her things ready for the morning. Her camera man was going to pick her up and take her to Maggie Andrews' house.

Chapter 6

Reggie rang the bell at Maggie's house the next morning, and it took a while for her sister Alice to look out the window by the door. When she saw it was Reggie she frowned, but opened the door.

The camera man had not started filming like he usually would have, but stayed back by the van in the street. Reggie knew that the minute they started filming without permission, Maggie's sister would throw a fit.

"I was hoping to talk to Mrs. Andrews and get her story about the explosion."

"Don't you get it?" Alice said with disgust. "If Maggie talks to you it will show exactly what she looks like and the street she lives on, and then you might as well draw a map to her home."

"But I have not told anyone about the white car. If she talks about what it was like to be there, I can bury that detail for now."

"Bury the detail. We have already had reporters calling the house, asking about 'the bomber.'"

"This is her chance to say she does not know what happened, and not mention any bomber, white car, or other detail that she wouldn't want released yet."

"You mean this is your chance to have her give you an exclusive. Safety is damned."

Alice was just about to close the door in Reggie's face when Maggie gently put her hand on her arm and opened the door.

"It's fine, Alice. I'll speak with this woman," she said firmly, stepping in front of Alice.

***

Reggie was taken aback by all the cuts on Maggie, and it must have showed on her face.

"I don't care what I look like. I'm awake and dressed, and I'm not going to lie. I don't know if there was a bomber, I don't know if it was an accident, but I'm just going to tell them that I'm alive and thankful for that. Maybe if I say I saw a white car, someone else might have as well. I'm not afraid of someone coming after me. That is absurd. No one is going to come looking for me, especially if I say I wasn't sure who exactly got in the car, except for it being a man, I think."

"Oh, so you did see someone?" Reggie said with slight excitement in her voice.

"Just that it was a white man, not tall or short, with wavy brown hair. I was too far away to see details, or with the explosion and my concussion, I have forgotten them." Maggie was getting tired of describing the person, and she sure couldn't trust her memory to be crystal clear with a head injury.

By now the neighbors were starting to come out to look

at the Channel 21 news van. Some of them may have heard what went on after seeing the news, or from her neighbor and friend Lila. But a few could be heard asking, "Why are they at Maggie's house? What happened?" The cameraman was then given the signal, and he came down the walk, starting to film Maggie.

Screw this, Maggie thought. *If I'm going to do this, it will be on my terms.* She grabbed her sister's arm to help her walk a little down the sidewalk as she heard Reggie starting to give a summary of yesterday's events.

"And now, Mrs. Andrews, I'm sorry this has happened to you. Can you tell our viewers about the explosion?"

Maggie looked directly into the camera. "All I know is that I was going by some offices when my car had a blowout. I went back to one of the buildings with a light on to use the phone, and that is when there was an explosion."

"Did you see anything odd or see someone?"

"I did notice a white car when I drove by with no front license plate."

"Did you see who was driving the car?"

"No, there was no one in the car at first, but right before the explosion I saw a man come out of the building."

Maggie suddenly had a flash of long curly hair on the man, and the almost "I'm in no rush" way he got into the car. She did not want to say this on the news. She knew that she was trying to be tough and brave, but she also knew that the smart thing to do was not to say anything more, at least to this reporter. Maybe to Detective Pierce, but not the reporter. She may as well put a bull's eye on her shirt that said, "I saw you, come get me."

"No, I did not see what the person looked like at all, and did not see a license plate, so I'm not much help. I don't even know what kind of businesses were along that strip except for the blinds place."

Maggie started to get a little weary and leaned on Alice. Reggie saw her fatigue and thanked Maggie for talking to her, and said she knew all her viewers were wishing Maggie well and to have a speedy recovery...and that if someone did do this they should hopefully be caught. What Reggie did not say on camera was that there were probably many viewers who were scared out of their wits thinking if there was someone out there, was it an isolated instance or something more?

"Thanks, Mrs. Andrews. I really do hope you get better. Can we talk again?"

"Please, call me Maggie," Maggie said. Reporter or not, there was something very likable and friendly about this girl. She was not that many years older than her sons. And she knew she was just doing her job. Alice was not very happy, but Maggie knew if she was going to talk to any reporter, she would rather it be Reggie. Maggie started to see other vans start to converge on her home for a story, so she invited Reggie and her cameraman into her home, but asked that no filming be done. She shut the door, avoiding the other reporters as they rushed up her walkway to get a story.

***

Maggie made one mistake. She had been so focused on the interview that she did not look at the crowd that had gathered in front of her house, or she would have noticed that one of the onlookers had long curly hair, and stood with a smug look of confidence and relief. Ten minutes after she had gone into the house, he turned to walk away with the crowd...fitting in with the crowd...fitting in VERY well.

CHAPTER 7

Mike saw the report on Mrs. Andrews on the news as he was getting ready for his shift, and thought she handled herself with class. He did not like that the interview took place in front of her home, and if she was involved in something that could cause her harm, this news report would lead them right to her.

His first order of business was to check out the businesses in the strip mall and see if they had any hazardous material that may have been stored there that could have caused the explosion. Maybe there wasn't a man in a white car. Who knew what a hit on the head could do? He did not want to tell her that, but who knew what the actual facts could be? She had said that she'd seen the white car by the end office, and a very faint light coming from the office window. The investigating team would know by today what kind of materials exploded, and if it was an accident.

Mike headed to work, and the place was busy with the

usual police business that went on during the day. Mike's sheriff said his priority was this case, and to keep an eye on Mrs. Andrews to see if she really was a victim or maybe a suspect.

"Hey George, any names yet on the businesses in the strip mall?" Mike asked, leaning over his desk.

George, a tall, round, teddy bear of a man, looked up from his work and said, "Of course, had them a while ago. You must be moving slow today, Mike."

Mike laughed and took the sheet of paper George handed him.

"Five businesses: A store that makes copies, computer fix-it shop, blinds store, siding company, and a glass company," Mike said out loud. "Which business is on the end, George?"

"Which end?" George asked.

"The first office you come to on the left side."

"That would be a store that sells blinds," George said, glancing at the piece of paper. "We have already contacted the owner of the store and the other four businesses that were damaged by the explosion. They will be coming in here today for formal interviews. Hope you can be around to talk to them and get a sense of what happened, and whether one of them drives a white car. The blinds store received the most damage, but the others received fire, water, and other damage…it's a mess. It still could be a gas leak, insurance fraud, or just one of those accidents that happen, but everyone was lucky no one was hurt. I want to get a list of their customers."

Mike said, "Let me know when the owners come in. I'll be at my desk looking up some information on their businesses and them. The task force probably will meet with them too. I want to stop by and see how Maggie is doing."

"So it's Maggie, is it? Doesn't hurt that she's pretty, huh,

Mike?" George said with a sparkle in his eye.

Mike felt his face get red, and said, "This is my case, George. You know that I never mix my work with women."

As he said it, he realized that he did notice Maggie was pretty, but noticed more that she seemed like she had a kind heart by her smile, and would not let anyone boss her around, which he admired in women. Annie had been kind, but God help anyone who tried to boss her around.

"Sure, Mike," George said, forcing himself to keep a straight face.

Mike went back to his desk. His partner was already at his own desk, on the phone, typing something into his laptop.

"Thanks. If you have anything else please let us know." He hung up the phone and turned to Mike.

"It looks like our accident theory is out the window, Mike," Wilson said, his face suddenly getting white as a piece of chalk. "They just finished their initial investigation, and it looks like it was some kind of explosive device. The only reason they know that is that one of their guys used to be special ops, and when no one could find anything, he saw one tiny spec of something and said, 'Oh, shit. We are in trouble.' This was a sophisticated device. In fact, they have not seen this type locally, EVER. The sheriff is calling in the FBI and someone from ATF from our closest regional offices. What I can't figure out is why someone would blow up a little business, in this tiny town, and be smart enough to use something like accelerant to have us think it was pure and simple arson? They probably had no idea that one of our guys could spot one tiny, tiny piece of something and know it was a bomb." Detective Wilson leaned over closer to Mike. "Mrs. Andrews may be in more trouble than she knows, or she may be more trouble than she looks. I think it is time we consider putting someone at her house for her protection. If it is okay with you, I will clear it with the captain and you can talk to her and explain without scaring her to death."

"Scaring her?" Mike said, shaking his head. "The minute she hears that there was a bomb and that she may really be in danger, she will freak out. She said she and her sister are leaving in ten days for a vacation about an hour away at that tourist's island. Good luck trying to keep track of her. We could order her not to leave the city, but let's just see how things play out. I don't like the fact that someone knows she was there. They are probably long gone, but I still think she deserves to know what really happened," Mike said as he put his hand through his short, curly blond hair, as he did when he was nervous or thinking hard. His ocean green eyes darkened as he thought about the case and about Maggie. He hoped that the higher ups let him tell her, but if a "pro" was on the loose, they didn't want word getting out. They probably would say to tell her it was arson. She would be scared, but not as scared as hearing that a person who had access to a sophisticated bomb might not be too happy with her.

"Let's go over there this afternoon and talk to Mrs. Andrews about this after we and the agents interview the business owners. I hope they kept back up files of all their customers, and they all did not go up in smoke with the explosion."

Oh, God, Mike thought, *how do we not let this get out to the media?*

When the team met that afternoon they told everyone to keep it quiet until they had a plan. He knew that Reggie was not the kind of woman that made up stories, but if the bomber thought Maggie might know something, she was in real danger.

Mike's phone rang as George let him know the first of the business owners were in the waiting area, and Jane from the task force was going to be joining Mike and his partner in the interview room. Mike wondered if anyone had a beef with one of the owners. If so, it sure must have been a complicated battle.

George also said the sheriff had approved putting someone on Maggie's street to keep an eye on her house, given that they now knew it was a bomb and not a gas leak.

Chapter 8

Maggie was so glad to be at home, and even happier that this happened way before their vacation. She may be the only person at the pool of the hotel with scratches and bruises, but she was not going to let anything ruin her dream trip with her sister. She had been to this resort with her husband for their honeymoon, and the thought of going back there with her sister made her feel happy: clear water, lots of sun, good food, and being able to remember the happy feelings she had there before with Henry. She had taken time off from being a social worker after her husband's death, and was planning to go back someday. In the meantime, she was doing volunteer work. It was great for taking time off like this. She did not have to worry about being on call or getting someone to cover her patients while she was gone. Her sister had her own business, so she was able to get more time off to go with Maggie, and had good managers to watch the business.

Maggie decided she was going to watch television all

day and pick DVD movies that were set in a forest and had pictures of blue water, to forget how horrible the past twenty-four hours had been. Her sister asked her if she wanted to cancel the vacation, but she already knew Maggie would say, "Hell, no." Maggie was not much of a drinker, but the thought of sitting by the pool with a wonderful rum drink called a Painkiller made her body feel better already.

The phone rang and she knew that it must be one of her sons. It was a real role reversal to have them call worried about her. They had wanted to come down to see her immediately, but Maggie did not want them here. She needed to rest, and knew that they were busy with their lives. She did tell them she would chat with them by webcam on the computer, as they had been very upset and wanted to see how she was doing.

"Hello."

"Hi, Mom," Allen said. "How are you?"

"They can't keep an old social worker down," she said lightly. Then she realized that she needed to tell them how she really felt. A part of her just wanted to protect them and forget this ever happened. She wanted to go back to just chatting about their lives and friends, and tell them more about her trip with their aunt. "Actually, Allen, I'm exhausted. This has been very scary for me, but I'm taking good care of myself, and your aunt is the perfect nurse for me. "

"I'll feel better when I can see you," Allen said, concerned. "What time do you want to go online and chat?"

"I'll call you after my nap this afternoon. I wish I wasn't such a dinosaur on the computer or I would know how to conference call you and your brother."

"No problem. We all have this program, so I will walk Aunt Alice through it to get you on. I'll call Todd and check with him regarding his schedule."

"So, is there anything new and exciting, Allen?" Maggie asked, hoping to change the topic.

"Work is good. I got out at five yesterday, which after working days till eight was like a vacation. We went to a new place that had great food and draft beers on tap."

"Hope you didn't have too much beer," Maggie said, taking on her mother role again.

"No, Mom, I didn't," Allen said, with his "Oh, no, here my mom the social worker goes again" voice. "No substance abuse here yesterday," he laughed, probably also glad to hear his mom was about to give him one of her "mom" speeches on the no texting while driving or no drinking and driving.

"Good to know. Talk to you later. Be warned that I'm a little beat up with cuts, scrapes, and bruises, but I am okay. Your aunt is keeping an eye on me for any concussion side effects. I have only had to take ibuprofen and I'm not in too much pain. My head hurts…no comment," she laughed, "but otherwise I'm fine. Please warn your brother if I don't talk to him first so he knows about the cuts and bruises."

"I will. Love you, Mom; we'll talk to you later."

"Love you too, Allen."

Maggie hung up the phone and told Alice about the call later and that she would need her help. She was suddenly hungry for lunch, but was really tired and just wanted to sleep after her lunch. She ached and would like a warm shower, but later on.

About three o'clock in the afternoon she woke up to the doorbell ringing. She had been so sound asleep that she was like a little kid, and had drooled on her pillow.

Alice answered the door and came back to tell Maggie that it was the officer from the hospital. Maggie said to let him in, and asked if Alice could get her a wash cloth so she could wipe her face.

She slowly crawled out of bed, trying to ignore the aches and pains, washed her face, and combed her hair. Really, for having survived an explosion, she was lucky she did not have more injuries, and the cuts were not deep at all, just scrapes. The bruises where she had fallen back were mostly covered by her clothes, and had started turning that nasty reddish purple color. The lump at the back of her head was there, but that would go down too.

Maggie walked out into the living room and saw Detective Pierce smiling at her. There was something about this man that made her feel comfortable, and pissed her off at the same time. Maybe it was his eyes, but it didn't hurt that he was about her age and handsome.

"Hello, Mrs. Andrews. I was hoping I could take a few minutes of your time. I wanted to see how you were doing, if you remembered anything new, and I also have some new developments in the case."

"Hello, Detective. Please sit down," she said as she motioned to the big comfy couch her husband and sons liked to sit on. She walked slowly over to her comfortable chair and sat down. Maggie did not feel like any chit chat after she heard there were new developments. "What new developments, Detective? And please, call me Maggie."

"Our team did find out that the explosion was not an accident. It was intentional."

"Did that man in the white car do it?" Maggie asked, feeling fear creep up her spine.

"We think so, but it's too early to be sure. We are interviewing all the owners of those businesses and their employees, but so far no one there drives a white car. Are you sure you did not see him clearly?" Mike said, looking closely at her reaction.

Maggie sighed and thought, *Here we go again*. "He was average height, white, and had wavy brown hair." What suddenly came into Maggie's mind was far more important than how he looked. It was his arrogant attitude by the way he walked. He was sure of himself…yet he moved like a sleek cat, with quick movements.

"I have to ask you, Maggie. Did he see you at all?"

"I don't think so," Maggie said. "I had stepped off the path, but I can't say for sure. It all happened so fast."

Maggie was getting a little nauseous from the detective's questions. Years in the social work profession had made Maggie read what people were really saying. She didn't analyze friends, but in cases like this, she could tell the detective was holding something back.

"If he did see me, then I'm in danger, right?"

Mike hesitated, but looked Maggie straight in the eye. "Yes, you could be. In fact, we are going to have someone near your house just as a routine procedure to watch your house."

"'Routine procedure,' or do I need to be scared?" Maggie asked.

Alice and Maggie sat forward, waiting for the detective's answer.

"Yes, I would be cautious if I were you. No need to take any chances."

Maggie could feel herself becoming afraid, but the overwhelming feeling of anger was also upon her.

"So, this bastard blows up a building, and I have to be careful this psycho does not come after me. I'm the prisoner." Maggie said, looking the detective in the eye, her eyes blazing.

***

Mike knew that behind her anger was fear, but he also knew she would not settle for anything but the truth.

"We are doing all we can to find this guy, and we may be calling in other law enforcement to help us."

"Who else are you calling in?" Maggie asked as she shifted her position in the chair so she wouldn't lean on her tender spots.

Mike looked at her, hesitating for a moment about how much to reveal. He couldn't help his voice lowering and getting more serious as he answered, "FBI and ATF."

"What, FBI and the Bureau of Alcohol, Tobacco, and Firearms?" Both Alice and Maggie gasped at the same time. "Does that mean what I think it means? You mean, not only is this not an accident, but this is really a bad situation?"

"It is serious, Mrs. Andrews—I mean Maggie—but we will be doing all we can to catch the person who did this. In the meantime, we will keep an eye on you. I'm sure this person is long gone."

Mike did not want to tell her about the type of explosive, as it was confidential information.

***

Maggie was silent for a long time as she thought about all the implications, and her thoughts turned to making sure her sons did not become involved. It was one thing for her to be in danger, but not her sons.

"Okay, I agree to having someone watch the house. But I will not be a prisoner. My sister and I will do what we need to do for me to heal and for us to be on our way to take our vacation in the next three weeks. We have had our reservations at the hotel for the past year, and no maniac is going to stop us from going."

"I can't speak for the FBI, but are you sure you want to go

50

out of town at all?"

"I will feel better getting away from here, actually, and as you said, whoever did this is probably long gone and wants nothing to do with me. I can't imagine someone that just blew up a building sitting down to watch the news. I can't have my sons finding out about the FBI yet. I don't want them in the dark or in danger, but I need to think how I want to tell them."

"Your sons are in their early twenties, aren't they?" Mike said, glad that the topic was getting off Maggie's vacation.

"My sons are adults, but still in their twenties. Their dad died five years ago and they haven't gotten over that totally. They still feel they have to check in on me. And this accident has them concerned, of course. In fact, they are doing an online call later to really see how I'm doing," Maggie said, letting herself laugh a little. She, too, wanted to change the topic, as she could feel herself getting tense at the reality of all this. "Do you have children, Detective?" Maggie asked.

"No. My wife and I hoped to have children, but we didn't. I was one of those late in life to get married guys."

"Maybe you and your wife will adopt?" Maggie said, smiling at the detective, realizing how totally inappropriate it was to say that. She noticed his eyes, his deep sigh, and his look of sorrow.

"My wife died years ago, also suddenly," Mike said softly. "I guess being a parent wasn't in the cards for me."

"I'm so sorry," Maggie said, understanding all too well the pain of having someone you love die.

"She was the love of my life, but I guess that life has its own plans."

"I guess it does, Detective." Maggie's anger seemed to fade as she got up and asked Mike if he would like to have some cake. Maggie always had cake in the house, and it seemed to make her feel better to offer it to her friends. The detective wasn't her friend, but after she found out he too had lost a spouse, she felt some barrier she'd put up against him had been torn down.

"I would love some. I don't eat sweets often, so this is a great treat for me."

"Let me get it for you both," Alice said, smiling at Mike and Maggie as she headed for the kitchen.

***

"She seems like she has your back," Mike said.

"She does. She was my rock when my husband died. And besides, who else can tease me about how I look now except my kids? And she keeps me laughing."

Alice brought the cake back and they all sat making small talk until Mike stood up, took his plate to the kitchen, and thanked Maggie and her sister for it.

"I have to leave now, but I will check in with you again, and let you know if anything else is new."

"Thanks, Detective," Maggie said as she hobbled to the door to see him out.

There were no news trucks in front of the house as Mike walked to his car. He saw the security detail car down the street that was far enough away, but close enough to watch Maggie.

***

But what he didn't see, way down the street in the opposite direction of the security detail in the woodsy park, was the blond haired man, who looked like he was watching birds with binoculars. He turned them towards Maggie's door as she stood there with Mike…and that same man turned away and disappeared into the forest.

CHAPTER 9

Reggie felt her interview with Maggie had gone well, but she wanted to find out more. She knew the police had learned by now if it was an accident or deliberate. If she let one of the other news stations get the lead on this, she was "slipping." She headed over to the police department without her cameraman, and was trying to come up with a plan of how to find out more information without getting booted out of the police station.

Reggie was known in the city for her stylish clothes, hair, and what her friends called her Mediterranean Model look, but today Reggie wanted to at least get to Mike without being hounded by regular people who thought she was a celebrity. She always was nice to people, but today she was on a mission. She walked up the steps in her jeans and baggy sweater, her hair tied back in a ponytail. As soon as she got to the waiting area, which she had seen many times while looking for story information, she asked for Detective Pierce.

The police officer behind the desk asked her what her name was and typed it into the computer, glancing at Reggie, fully aware of who she was.

"I don't see any appointment scheduled. What did you say your business was with him?" she said, peering up at her.

"He said he might have some information on a case I'm working on." Reggie did embellish that last part, but she had worked on stories where Mike was the detective before and he did always come through.

"Let me call him," the officer said, picking up the phone. "Mike, this is Sarah. I have a woman here called Reggie Page, who said she needs to talk with you."

The officer waited for his answer, and buzzed Reggie in to go back to Mike's office.

"Thanks," Reggie said as she headed through the door.

She walked into Mike's office and he motioned for her to sit down. Neat it wasn't, but Mike seemed to have everything in order, making it easy for him to find what he needed.

"Hi Reggie, what can I do for you? Did you try the old 'I have an appointment with Mike today' routine?" he chuckled.

"Sure did. I knew that by now you would know more about the Andrews case. I have to go back with something new today or my boss will throw a fit."

Mike went from smiling to suddenly sighing deeply. "Reggie, I have nothing to add to the story. You know there was a white car and a man, but it could have been one of the business owners stopping by their store who just happened to leave before the explosion."

"So this wasn't deliberate?"

"I can't tell you anything more, Reggie. I can say that we are looking at all aspects of this, and have interviewed the business owners and some of the employees."

"Is there any money coming to any of them if their business is destroyed?" Reggie asked, sitting forward to wait for Mike's answer.

"We're checking on that, Reggie. As I find out or receive any information, I will let you know."

"Then tell me, were you able to get any video footage from that morning from the businesses, or is there anything odd you have found out?"

"What is odd, Reggie, is that most of the businesses did not have cameras, or the few that did had the video feed to a tape in their store. The ones they found were disintegrated in the explosion. But again, don't mention that detail. If someone did cause this we want them to think that they can't get away with it, and maybe they are on camera," Mike said, starting to stand up to signal that was all he would say.

Reggie just did not buy his story, and she could tell he was rattled by something. "So Maggie has been updated on the case?"

"Maggie is a nice woman, Reggie. I wouldn't press her too much for details. The less she can be on the news the better. She is still pretty banged up from the explosion and upset about it."

"She's a nice woman, Mike, but if someone is after her, she has a right to know that she is in danger. So please, when you find out anything tell her, and then text or call me on your smart phone and give me a scoop."

Reggie had seen Mike concerned about crimes and victims, but he seemed especially troubled about this. Reggie decided that he was holding back something, but she said her goodbyes to him and started out to the lobby. As she left she saw two men walk by her with dark suits and white shirts, headed towards Mike's office. *Feds*, she thought. *There IS more to this than an accident.*

Reggie kept her head down as they passed, but heard one say to the other, in almost a whisper, "He knows about the other bomb."

She held her breath for a second, then said, "Oh, damn, this is really bad," as she headed out the door. She did not want to run something that was not true, but she was a reporter.

She waited till she was out of the building and dialed Maggie's number. "Hi, this is Reggie Page. I appreciate you letting me come over this morning. I heard that there was new information. Can I come over again?"

Reggie heard Maggie's sister Alice turn away from the phone and ask Maggie. Alice said, "She does not want anyone to come today. You can come tomorrow. What new information?"

Reggie casually said, "The FBI?"

There was a stunned silence on the other end before Alice said, "Please don't mention any of that on the news. Maggie's life could be in danger."

"I won't be doing another story tonight, and I'll wait until we talk tomorrow," Reggie promised, suddenly realizing that her getting the story could get this woman hurt.

"Thank you so much," Alice said, almost breathing a sigh of relief. "We will see you tomorrow. How about in the morning? Maggie is the most rested then."

"That sounds good. See you tomorrow."

Reggie was going to go back to her office and work on some of the other stories that were coming in, but her mind was racing with thoughts of Maggie's story. When she got to her office, her boss called her in and filled her in on two breaking stories. One was a murder down near First Street, and the other was a break-in not far from where Maggie lived.

She decided to head to the murder scene, and tomorrow she would catch up on the break in when she went to see Maggie.

She grabbed her cameraman and headed downtown. It had just been called in, so she and one other station were the only ones there. She showed her reporter's badge to the detective in charge and stood the respectful distance that was required when filming a murder scene. The body was lying in a deserted parking lot, face down, with blood pooling from one side of the head. It looked to be a male dressed in a business suit, blond hair, and by what she could see of his face, in his thirties.

Must be a robbery, Reggie thought. She approached the lead detective and asked if there was any information she could give her. The detective's team was already examining the body.

The detective said, "We have found the body of a white male, approximately in his thirties, shot in a parking lot. We do not know the motive for the shooting, but we do know he has been dead for about four hours. There was no wallet or identifying information on the body, so we are getting fingerprints to try to identify the victim and notify his relatives. After we process the crime scene the medical examiner will do an autopsy to get a better sense of his death."

Reggie gave her cameraman the go ahead to start filming and began her reporting.

"This is Reggie Page, reporting to you on what was supposed to be one of our quieter streets, now the scene of a terrible tragedy."

As she was reporting, she saw the detective pull something out of the John Doe's inside suit jacket pocket. From a distance it looked like a business card, but she could not tell.

Poor guy. Murdered and left to die on a cold street, and the only thing left on him was a business card. This part of Reggie's job made her sad. A person just never knew how much time they had in life, and she hoped he had at least said "Have a good morning" to the people he loved.

Reggie finished her story and wanted to check in with her eleven o'clock team to see if they could get the victim's name before the news aired. They would have to call their contacts and see if anyone was willing to spill anything. She knew that family would have to be contacted first.

After jumping into the van, Reggie decided to call her parents. Her parents had their own business and would be there today. With the intense heat, their ice cream shop was the "hit" of the town. She hoped she called at a quiet time, not wanting to disturb them during business hours. She knew they would say a call from her would never be a disturbance, but that was her parents. Something about the last two days made her want to hear their voices, as sappy as that sounded to her.

The phone rang a few times before she heard her mom's cheerful voice.

"Hi, Reggie. I love when you call because your ring is Aretha Franklin's song 'Respect,' and that gets some of my customers happy and singing along. No one here now, though. How are you? Al, pick up the phone. It's Reggie."

"Fine, Mom. I just thought I would call and say hello."

"Reggie, you know I hate the word fine. Give me all the details. I love details." her mom laughed.

There was a click and her dad said, "Hello, Reggie."

"Hello, Dad."

"So how is the big city? Have you been on television a lot?" her mom asked.

"Well, actually, I have, Mom. If you log on to the station's link you can see my report."

"What did you cover?" her mom asked.

"It was an explosion. Don't worry, I'm fine. I just covered the story and I'm working on it."

"Oh my goodness. Was anyone hurt?"

"Not seriously, but one woman was near the explosion and got banged up pretty bad. I'll tell you more after you see the report. I just called to see how you and Dad were doing?"

"Terrific. Thank goodness it's been so hot, so business has been great. I'm overdoing it with ice cream myself, and have to cool it," her mom laughed…a laugh that made her sound like a delighted young child. "Your dad and I have done a few things with friends, but nothing else too new. We hope to come and visit you soon. I wish you were closer, but that's life. Are you staying safe?" her mom began again with her being safe mom lecture.

Something about it this time made Reggie smile and wish she could hug her mom in person.

"Yes, I'm safe. I have good friends, and of course I always keep my eyes open for the love of my life," Reggie laughed.

Her folks laughed and she could hear the bell of the store door opening.

"Talk to you later, Mom and Dad. Love you."

"Love you too, Reggie," they both chimed in.

After they hung up Reggie wished she had told them to be safe.

CHAPTER 10

Mike went back to the station and held a meeting with the team working on Maggie's case. He wanted to get some of the information they had found out about the businesses and start piecing together some kind of motive. Yes, the Feds were going to be involved, and this was a small town and they did not have all the sophisticated equipment that they showed on TV, but none the less, they were good at solving crimes by their team work. He, his partner, Edwin, Lee Ann, and Jim made up the detectives in the squad.

"So Jim, what did you find out about the businesses?"

Jim, a tall slim detective with a crooked smile and boyish appearance, went to the board and said, "We know there were five businesses. First business at the end was a computer store. They take in old computers and add memory, repair them, etc. It was the first tenant of the buildings. The owner has lived in our town for years with his wife, and has a grown son and his wife who are in town, too. He has never had any problems at the office before. Said he has never seen anything unusual, and there was nothing in his store that someone would want to blow it up for. Maybe break in and steal computers, but not blow it up. He seemed really genuinely upset, and confused. He had planned to come in at eight as usual and open up, but his wife was ill.

"Our second business is a blinds store. That's run by a man and his brother, and they go out to homes to fit blinds and then make and do repairs in their store. They have never had a theft, have clean records, and they open up at eleven. They could not think of anything someone would want to blow up their store for, and have no enemies that they were aware of.

"Our third business was a plumbing supply store. Again, they have been owners for many years, no criminal record, sell—plumbing. They said they go in at ten and have never had any problems or thefts, or enemies either. He was supposed to be in earlier, but believe it or not his pipe at home broke, so he did not make it. That leaves two that were supposed to be in earlier, so maybe they were a target.

"Our fourth business was an import business. The owner had a criminal record many years ago in his youth, but that was for dope, and he's had this business for years. He didn't think he has any enemies, but back in the day he had a few encounters with odd characters due to his doing dope. Now he has kids, a home in the city, and seems to have straightened out after his few months in jail. He did say that about two months ago he noticed a woman walk back and forth in front of all the stores, taking pictures of the water across from the stores, but he said she turned once and took a picture of his building. Must be a photography nut or tourist, he thought. Dumb tourist...as if this building is one you want to brag about, he remembered thinking at the time.

"Our fifth business was a glass store. The owner seems like a decent guy. Lives alone, and most of his days are spent at the shop. He seemed the most crushed of all the owners, and really looked to be in shock. They all said they loved their businesses, but they weren't millionaires. They had to put in tons of hours six days a week, and most times didn't mind. Their customers were loyal."

"Thanks, Jim. So did any of these people have their businesses insured?" Mike asked.

"Basic insurance," Lee Ann said.

"Will you do one more check to see what company insured them and for how much?"

"Do we need a warrant for that, Mike?"

Mike shook his head. "Did they say anything about new customers, or anyone coming around within the last two months with any big orders, complaints, etc.?" Mike asked.

"Only one time, one of the owners said. A lady came into the computer store and kept asking about prices of computers, which were the safest to protect information, and seemed very agitated. I asked what she looked like, and he said an attractive woman in her thirties but nervous, and she kept looking out the window," Lee Ann said.

"Did she buy anything"? Mike asked.

"No, she said she would have to think about it and left," Jim said. "He didn't get her name, just remembered her stopping in."

For an instant Mike's heart stopped as he thought, *I really hope that Maggie was telling the truth about all this. None of this makes sense. Why blow up a building with an extreme bomb? Why not just set it on fire, or better yet steal what it is you want destroyed? And why do it at a time when no one is there if you want payback?*

Mike thought for a minute then said, "Let's have Edwin

continue gathering information and seeing what connections everyone may have. See if anyone got out of jail recently that might have an explosives work background, and check out if we have anyone in town that was in the Special Forces. That one will probably come from Homeland, but we can see what we can get. Again, let's see if the owners were honest about what insurance they or their families stand to collect if something happens to their stores.

"We should also find out more from Homeland Security, as they have all the big 'stuff' to investigate with. They are adamant that we don't tell anyone about the bomb. They want to let the public think it was an accidental explosion, so remember…the truth stays in this room. No telling friends, family, or the media. Eventually it will get out, but let's give them at least a day to get leads and maybe nail this guy."

"Okay. And while you were gone we just had a murder called in downtown," Jim said. "A young guy was shot. No ID, nothing except a business card in his pocket and his briefcase with only papers in it. It must have been a mugging. We checked on him in our system from his business card, and when we put in his address, what was weird was we had a call come in on a break in at the address he was listed at."

"You say there were only papers in the case?" Mike asked.

"Yes, but we're dusting it now for fingerprints and running it through our computers. We have not had anyone call in as it has not been on the news yet, and no one has called in a missing persons report."

"Good, let me know when that all comes in," Mike said. "Where was it on the west side?"

"I believe Republic Street. If my memory serves me right, the break in was near Mrs. Andrews' house," Jim replied. "We think it was a pro. The only thing missing was an expensive laptop and a tablet. The tablet was in the dresser drawer by the jewelry, but only a few pieces of jewelry, two expensive watches, were taken. The watches were high end ones, so our burglar did not want to bother with TVs or low end jewels, just the stuff they could get rid of and make money fast.

"An alarm came through to the alarm company and they sent a squad car out to investigate. It took them longer to get there than expected. No one was in the house, but the back door was open and the window pane by the door was shattered. The detective did not know if the burglar was in the house, but after he and his partner checked out the place they called the owner."

"Any prints?" Mike asked.

"Not so far," Jim said, shaking his head. "Again, a professional. They were wearing gloves, left no shoe prints, and the place is as neat as if a housekeeper came."

"Were there any cameras around that area that might have caught a car, or did anyone see anything? Was there anything fenced today?" Mike asked, covering all bases.

"Andy is out checking out the neighborhood, nearby stores, and his pawn shop connections. We should know more tomorrow," Edwin said.

"Who are the owners of the house?" Mike asked.

Jim checked his notes. "A man named Carl, but he's out of the country and has been renting it to two guys, one of whom is our dead guy. Steve is who we spoke with. He's twenty-nine, never married, and moved into the house about two months ago from Boston to work at a downtown financial company. I called his office to speak with him, and he came right home. That is how we knew about the laptop, jewelry, and electronic notebook.

"Steve seemed very shocked about this, and had no idea

his roommate was murdered or why. He could not figure how someone could take his things so fast. We asked him if there was anything on his or his roomie's computers that we should know about, or the one in his drawer. He had a funny look on his face, but said nothing special, just a little porno on his tablet...all legal, of course. He couldn't speak for his roomie, since Steve had just moved in two months ago, and really did not know his roommate very well. His roommate used to live in a one bedroom apartment, but wanted more space. They met on an online roommate search site."

"Let's check into the actual owner a little more. I wonder why he's out of the country. Did you ask Steve?"

"No, I didn't," Jim said, shaking his head, "but I will be checking back with him. He's getting a glass company to fix the back window pane once our guys process it."

Mike suddenly felt an alarm go off in his head. "What glass company?"

"I don't know. Why does it matter?"

"Second time today I heard the word glass company, and it would be a hell of a coincidence if it was the glass company that burned that he was calling."

"I doubt it, Mike, but I'll find out."

Mike checked the time, and as usual he would be getting out late. In some ways it did not bother him to stay at work now that his wife was gone. With no one to go home to, he did not mind working extra hours. They closed the pool late, so he could always take a swim later on. He loved Chinese food, so the people in a nearby restaurant delivered to him at least three times a week. They knew his order by heart, and when his moo shu chicken or his lo mein came, he tipped them well. He missed sitting at the table with his wife in the family room, eating their food, laughing and catching up on each other's day. At least at the office there was the buzz of activity that made his life not seem so empty. Maybe he should get a pet, his friends said, but he wasn't ready for that yet.

Mike's phone rang and it was his boss, the sheriff, telling him that the Feds wanted Mike to be lead detective on the case for the unit and work with them in this. They were in the process of getting fingerprints, looking at cameras, seeing if any bomb equipment had been purchased in their town, and a million other things that Mike would probably never know about. Hell, they were probably checking him out to make sure Mike was on the up and up.

His boss said they wanted him to keep in contact with Maggie every few days if possible, and to keep the protection on her.

"Sure boss, I can do that." Mike thought he would be doing that anyhow as he felt Maggie could be in danger, and frankly they hadn't totally ruled her out as a suspect.

Mike headed home, and managed to get in a swim and have a beer and chips. He looked around his place before he fell asleep. Everything was in perfect order. The damn place was too clean, too orderly, and missing something…or really someone. "It isn't perfect at all," he sighed, as he drifted off with his heart feeling empty.

CHAPTER 11

Maggie rested all the next week, feeling stronger every day. Neighbors stopped in with casseroles for her and her sister. She basked in the sun in her bedroom as she took her daily naps with her cat. In between all that her sister and her would watch television, laugh, and sit on the back deck, soaking in the late afternoon sun. She got an "all clear" from her doctor at her one week follow-up appointment, and that eased her mind tremendously.

Each day she had a call from Detective Mike, as she called him now, and he was going to come over and give her an update. She heard from her sons briefly each day, and her fear of someone trying to "get her" were lessening. Nothing to do with her, she would tell herself. She needed to get herself well and her balance back before she and her sister left on their trip. Her sons volunteered to visit, and even help her on the trip, but she assured them that she was healing, and the trip would be a great way to end this horror she and her sister had been through. Her good friend would watch her cat, Bailey, while she was gone. Reggie did a nice job of not focusing on Maggie on the news, but giving updates that there were no leads in the bombing. She called regularly and once stopped in, only telling Maggie that she herself was looking into any leads from her "sources." The sheriff did not want any information given out by Reggie, so the details of the type of bomb that the ATF was investigating were only shared with the police and FBI.

Maggie knew they were involved, but she did not know any details. Usually she would "bug" people with questions until she found her answers, but she was not up to it. She wanted the law enforcement detectives to do that. Also, physically she was recovering, but her having a night where she was not waking up in a cold sweat with PTSD would take a while. Maggie felt she was a lot clearer now, and when Mike came over she could possibly remember more details.

The next day at noon Detective Mike stopped by, and Maggie felt flushed as she realized her attraction to him as he walked up her sidewalk. She had known he was coming, so she had put on an extra layer of lipstick, and a teal blue loose top with her loose sweat pants. She was still bruised and swollen and had scrapes, but they too were healing.

The doorbell rang and Maggie yelled, "I'll get it." She opened the door and Mike stood there with a bag in his hand.

"Thought you might want something for lunch, and this burger place is my favorite grab and go place in the area. I should have asked if you eat fast food, but I took a chance."

The smell of a burger and french fries made Maggie smile. Her husband sometimes would bring home burgers and fries, and they would devour them as they caught up on each other's days.

"This is perfect. I have some watermelon we can cut up,

TOO LATE TO RUN

and some coffee I just made. Let's go eat it on the back porch. It's not too hot yet, and we can enjoy some fresh air."

They settled in at the table as Alice joined them for lunch.

"Any updates yet?" Maggie asked.

"We continue to investigate. We don't know which business our bomber was targeting or why, but we will find out. We did find out that there was a break-in in town, and the owner of that house had used the glass company in the past to repair his car window."

"So you think it is the glass company that was the target?" Maggie asked after slowly swallowing a bite of her burger.

"We are checking into that. Now Maggie, you said that you had never been to the businesses before, is that correct? What about the blinds store?" Mike asked, scanning Maggie's face for her answer.

"As I told you before, detective, years ago we had a blinds company put our vertical blinds in our home, but I did not go to the store, they came out to the house. They came out to measure our windows, made them, and then installed them."

Maggie quickly realized that she was not totally off the hook, and there was some suspicion on the detective's part that she could be involved. She was annoyed, because of course she could never be involved, but she could see by using the blinds company she may be a person of interest.

"Detective," she said, bristling a little. "I had nothing to do with this explosion, and I seriously doubt that having a blinds company come out years ago makes me an accessory in the bombing."

"I'm not saying that, but I have to check out everything," Mike said, seeming a little annoyed by Maggie's attitude.

"Okay, truce," Maggie said, suddenly trying to lighten the mood. "Let's just eat our burgers and fries, and I will answer any more questions you have later. So tell me about yourself, Detective," Maggie said in her best social worker voice.

Mike smiled, his dimple showing this time, and said, "Okay, okay, I get it, your turn. Well, my mom and dad are still living in Michigan. My mom's a teacher in South Lyon and my dad does consulting work in Ann Arbor. They hoped that I would become a teacher, but I had an uncle who was a cop and he used to spend a lot of time at our home. I always wanted to hear the stories of him getting the 'bad guys,' and I guess from then on I was hooked. For five years I was married to a wonderful woman named Annie, as you know, and she was taken from me by an aneurysm. I have no kids, like to swim, love animals, and am a big *Star Wars* fan. I'm a good cook, but if I'm on a case that consumes most of my time. End of story. That's my life."

"I'm sorry about your wife," Maggie said, feeling her own heart hurt a little for him. "I lost my husband to a heart attack a few years back, as you know, and it still hurts."

They both were silent for a few minutes as they finished their lunch, and Alice got up to take the dishes to the kitchen, feeling sad for them both.

"I have to get back to the office. I will check in with you this week. I still am not certain it is a good idea for you to leave on a vacation," Mike said somewhat sternly.

"Detective, whoever placed the bomb is not going to come after me here, let alone on an island. I'm going out in the car for the first time today with Alice, and even into a store. I will be fine."

Maggie really did believe that all this was coming to an end, and that no person would be foolish enough to come after her. It was not like she could identify them. Then she would be in danger, but Reggie had been great at reporting that she saw nothing of the bomber except that he was average height and had dark wavy hair. She was too far away to see his eyes or facial features...just his arrogant walk....

***

Mike got up and started to walk to the door with Maggie. As he walked out the door, he turned and saw Maggie's crystal blue eyes and her serious-face, which made him feel an overwhelming desire to take her in his arms and hold her, telling her all would be all right. Of course he would not do that, and he would have no physical contact with her, but it was the first time in a long time he had felt like this...actually, the first time since Annie.

"Bye, Maggie."

"Bye, Detective Mike," she laughed, and kept looking at his eyes until he broke eye contact and turned and walked down the walkway.

Mike spotted the car watching her house, and at least felt good that she had some protection. He knew she was not as worried anymore, or hid it well, but he had a bad feeling that something big was going on that she had no clue about. Across the street and two houses down, Mike noticed a utility guy fixing the phone wires.

***

If he had been closer he may have noticed the small indentation on the pole, and a shiny camera in it.

He wouldn't know that someone had a wonderful view of Maggie's front yard and her garage from that tiny pinhole camera they'd planted. "Ah, modern technology," the bald man with a mustache and a cap would chuckle later that day, sitting in his lounge chair as he sipped his whiskey and smoked his cigar, eyeing his monitor on the table.

Chapter 12

Maggie walked to the kitchen after she had shut the front door. Alice was putting things away and turned and gave her the biggest grin.

"He is cute, isn't he, Maggie? If I had to have someone be my protector, it would be him."

Maggie grinned. "Yes, he is cute, but remember he's a detective, and all he cares about, I hope, is finding out why that person blew up the building. I'm really not worried about this person coming after me, but I worry something could happen to my boys. I want to keep them as far away as possible. They were both a little shook up when they saw me on Skype the other day, but they weren't as freaked out last night. I really need to be honest with them, but there is part of me that does not want them to know about Homeland Security and the FBI being involved. They would have me go stay with them, or want to rush here, and I don't want that. I want them to be informed and be aware if there is any danger."

Maggie's stomach lurched at the slim possibility that maybe she really was still in this nightmare, and was still in danger.

"Oh Alice," she said giving her sister a hug. "I'm frightened a little."

Alice hugged her quietly for a minute and said, "I know you are, Maggie. That's why I'm here."

Maggie pulled away and said, "Okay, sis, I'm ready for my second car ride. I can't wait to go to the grocery store."

They got their things together and headed out to Alice's car. Maggie still had to walk slower than usual, and of course still had aches and painful bruising, but she felt a sense of relief just getting out. She waved to her neighbor across the street and felt for a second that it was like any other day, and she and her sister were going out shopping.

She yelled, "Thanks for the casserole, Lila. It was delicious, and you're spoiling me."

Lila had always been one of her best friends besides a neighbor, and she also had two sons who now lived on the other side of town. The boys would either play at her or Lila's home growing up, and Maggie still sometimes missed the fun of the water balloon fights, endless pizzas, and good times they all had.

Lila was married to Ted, who traveled a lot and been one of her husband's best friends. Sometimes their husbands would go off by themselves to have their "guy time" away from the women and kids. The four of them would get together often, and Lila was a wonderful cook. Maggie had never been fond of cooking. She had to cook when the guys were home, but it was her husband who loved to putter in their kitchen and come up with his creations.

Maggie and Alice got in the car and started on their

adventure, laughing like school girls at Maggie's being thrilled to go to a grocery store. As they left Maggie's street, she suddenly turned to Alice and said, "Would you mind if we go the back way to the store? I might be able to remember something if I go by where the explosion took place...and besides, I have to face it sometime. I may get a little faint or feel nauseous, but I'll have you there."

"I don't know," Alice said, frowning, hands tightening on the steering wheel. "I know you're a mental health person, but I'm not sure you're ready, Maggie."

"Please, Alice, I need to do this."

"Okay," Alice said, obviously not feeling it was okay at all. "But we are not stopping."

"Deal, we won't stop."

They turned down Temple Street and were close to the bombing site. Maggie didn't say a word, and you could have heard a pin drop as they approached the site. It looked like what she'd seen on television when they showed places damaged by tornados...crushed, burnt. There were two bulldozers at the site now with one big dump truck, trying to clear out the debris.

Instead of Maggie getting nauseous, she became strangely focused and tried to remember anything she could. Being a passenger now, she was able to really take in the area and sights in a way she had not done before. She asked Alice to slow down a little, and would have jumped out for a closer look if she had not promised her sister she would stay in the car. Alice had been so terrific with her that she did not want to upset her.

Yet, as she rode by she could almost smell the smoke and hear the explosion again. That was posttraumatic stress kicking in, but when they drove a little further and she saw a piece of her blown out tire on the road, she was overcome with feelings. She got a picture of her walking back to the business with the light on, and some guardian angel must have had her stop before the explosion. If she had been going at her regular fast pace, she might have gotten further and might not be there today. That made Maggie very sad suddenly, and as they drove she thought not about her being gone, but her sister and sons' grief....

Alice quickly turned to her and back to the road. "I know a lot is going through your head, Maggie, but I'm so glad you're still here. Whoever did this had a grudge against someone, but not you. They got whatever they wanted by blowing it up, and I would be more worried if I owned one of those businesses."

"You're right, Alice," Maggie said. "Maybe I can help Detective Mike with some of this."

"Come on, Maggie," Alice said, annoyed. "I thought you were coming to terms a little with this, but now you are talking about helping with this crime. You were almost killed, and are still covered with bruises. Give me a break."

"Okay, okay, just a thought. I guess I felt I should be a part of getting this bad guy, but you're right, it is a bad idea. I need to get well, keep all of us safe, and we need to go to the island resort and relax. Let Detective Mike and his group solve this one. Of course, I wouldn't mind if Detective Mike helped to protect me," Maggie said with a light laugh in her voice, which got Alice laughing as she responded.

"I bet you wouldn't mind."

Maggie loved going out to the grocery store and just walking around. They filled up the cart with all sorts of goodies that they both liked, and sampled some of the cheeses and soups that the store employees were giving out.

They checked out after Alice ran to get one more bottle

of wine, and started for the parking lot. Basket full, they both stopped for a moment to remember where they had parked. Maggie's car was older and did not have the automatic keyless entry. They were headed down one of the main aisles when Alice pointed to their car in the opposite direction. Maggie and Alice turned their cart down one of the other aisles when suddenly a car sped by, missing them and their cart by just a fraction, and Alice tumbled to the ground. Maggie gasped and helped Alice up.

"Are you okay?"

"I'm fine, but I'm furious. This happens to me in my parking lot occasionally. Some jerk was probably on their cell phone and in a rush to go nowhere. The jerk did not even bother to come back and see if we were okay. Good thing you turned the cart to go in another direction, or we could have been seriously hurt," Alice said.

"But we are okay," Maggie said, "so let's go home and not let this ruin our outing. What a jerk. I couldn't see if it was a man, woman, or teen, could you?"

"Not at all," Alice said.

They loaded the car with the groceries and headed home, their anger fading.

Maggie was glad Alice did not look at her face while they drove, because she would have seen the frown above her brow. That was her "sign" that she was worried.

Maggie shuddered inside as she couldn't help but think what an odd thing they were almost run down…she prayed there was no connection to the last few weeks.

Chapter 13

Mike hung up the phone and looked up to see Reggie at his office door.

"Hi, Mike, just checking in on the explosion case. Are there any new leads?"

"Well, what I can tell you is that the homicide that you were covering has some connection. The man shot dead, his name was Alan Tuber. He had a card at his home for the computer business that was blown up. We're thinking maybe he had something to do with the explosion, but we don't know what. We traced his fingerprints through every system we use, and even the FBI ran them through theirs, but no criminal matches. Just an average guy who worked as a financial analyst, who had a business card from the place that was blown up, and his wallet was gone. There are no records to look up on the buildings, and the computer company had no back up files."

Reggie said, "I'm surprised there were no cameras in the area where the man was shot that captured something."

"We're looking at other camera footage, but it will take time. Not for public knowledge, Reggie, but we did find out that the shooter was not at street level, but from somewhere higher."

"So this was a pro?"

"I can't say. Our guys are looking at this, and also seeing if there is any connection to the explosion."

"Think this is a onetime explosion, or should we be worried?" Reggie said quietly, leaning closer to Mike.

"Let's hope this was a onetime thing. Please don't let anyone get the idea that there could be more bombs, or we will have a town in panic."

"It kills me to hold this back, Mike, but I will because of Maggie. I'm going over to her house now. She leaves next week, and I want to see if she's heard anything. I wish she was not going out of town, but hey, I can tell she's stubborn."

"See you, Reggie. I have to get back to this case and I have a meeting soon," he said, getting up from his desk.

***

Just as Reggie was about to walk out of the office, a tall dark-haired man walked into the room.

"Hey, Sam, would you please walk Reggie to the stairs?"

Reggie was about to protest, but Sam looked into her eyes for what seemed like a long time and grinned.

"Of course. It's not every day that I get to escort a famous reporter out of the building."

"You've seen me on television?"

"Are you kidding?" Sam said as they walked down the hall. "I watch your reports whenever I can. You're not a cut throat reporter or Suzie Sweet either, but you tell it like it happens." As they got to the door and Sam opened it for Reggie, he asked, "Are you coming back to get more on this story?"

"Absolutely," she said, feeling that they both had more than the story in mind.

"If I'm not being too forward, how about going to dinner with me and you can tell me about the world of reporting?"

Reggie was a little taken aback by his boldness, but the shakiness in his voice as he asked made her realize he was as nervous as her.

"Sure, I would love that. Where would you like to meet? How about Andy's? They have a nice menu, and it is not too noisy to talk."

Reggie loved Andy's, and was glad she had suggested meeting somewhere because, cop or not, she did not like people picking her up at her place until she'd known them awhile.

"Sounds great. How about seven tomorrow, or is that too early?"

"Just right, Sam," Reggie said, almost melting when she looked into his gorgeous eyes and kind, handsome face. "See you then."

Reggie had not felt an instant attraction to anyone in a long time, but she sure felt it now.

She wondered if her cheeks were flushed as she left the building. It had been a long time since she had felt herself almost actually lusting after someone…too long.

***

Reggie headed over to Maggie's house and saw her in the front yard, grabbing groceries out of the trunk with Alice.

"Hey, I thought you were supposed to be resting," Reggie teased.

"Me?" Maggie said, feeling good to be bantering with someone again, and feeling at ease with Reggie. "Help me take a few bags in, Reggie, and I might make you something to eat."

"It's a deal, but I'm here on business. Can I do a follow-up for the news on how you're doing?"

Maggie hesitated, but said that was fine if Reggie made it short, and did not mention any more personal things that the public might not know. She knew the other stations were trying to get a story, but there was something about Reggie, so she did not mind speaking with her. If she had a daughter, she would want her to be honest and funny like Reggie. Too bad her sons were in different cities, or she would play a matchmaking mom.

"Sure. Do you want to do it now and get it over with? Plus, your cameraman deserves a sandwich."

"That would be great."

Reggie had her cameraman come out of the van to shoot the piece. Maggie seemed glad the interview would be low key, as Reggie had promised her. Maggie complimented the city's police department and said she had recovered well, and was sure that the police would get whoever set the bomb. She knew to give Reggie only what she needed and no more. After the interview, Reggie said she would come in for a quick bite to eat, but needed to get this back to the station.

As they all sat around, munching on their sandwiches and chips, there was an ease between them. Alice mentioned their near miss in the parking lot. It was Reggie who became serious this time, and said to Alice and Maggie, "You're lucky. Things come in threes, they say. Let's not try for another injury." Reggie was about to drop the subject, but said, "Do you think it was intentional, ladies?"

"Oh, no," Maggie said, almost too quickly. "You know how this can happen sometimes in a parking lot, especially if someone is on their cell phone and not paying attention."

"That happens sometimes to me too, Maggie. I just had to ask. I wish you would rethink your trip next week, until this maniac is caught."

"Alice and I will be safe. The place is a lovely resort an hour away, and it is on an island. It will be a great place to rest and forget about this mess, and just let loose a little."

"I know it sounds great. I guess I'm just a little concerned," Reggie said.

Maggie could tell Reggie was genuinely worried. "Okay, Reggie, you could use a little rest and relaxation, so why don't you come along? You could have fun, and then you wouldn't worry about us while we're gone. No cameras allowed."

"Very funny," Reggie chuckled. "Can you imagine me on a vacation? I've been here a year, and besides seeing my folks briefly, haven't been on a vacation. With my luck a story would come up on vacation, and compulsive me would feel I had to cover it. I know, workaholic to the bone."

"I was half serious, Reggie," Maggie said. "Alice, would you mind if we had our own news girl along?"

Alice laughed and said, "I'm in. How many times can we vacation with a television star? And besides, you could tell your boss you are doing a human interest story on us when all this is figured out, and you'll have the photos to prove it."

"Great idea," Reggie laughed. "I'll think about it."

Reggie and her cameraman finished their sandwiches and headed to the office to get afternoon work done.

CHAPTER 14

Reggie did think about going on vacation, and when she met her girlfriends later for their dinner, they all thought it was a great idea. They had no idea what was going on with the case, except what Reggie had said on the news. She felt bad not telling them about some of the details, or warning them that that there could be another bomb somewhere, but she had promised Mike and wanted to protect Maggie. She reassured herself that the maniac probably had a grudge against one of the businesses, and it would end there. She hoped they could narrow it down to which business, and what if anything the dead man had to do with the case.

"Go. Go and relax. I've heard the resort is fantastic, and maybe your boss will pay your costs for you to cover the story," her friends said.

"Hey," Reggie said, "even if he pays only half of it that would be great."

Reggie laughed and caught up on her friend's lives as

they sipped their wine. When she briefly mentioned Sam and how they were going to meet for dinner tomorrow, they all laughed and said she should go to the police department more often. All except her neighbor, Carol, who scowled and said "Be careful, you never know what he's hiding."

Reggie laughed and said she was more concerned about his good looks.

"I wish someone would have warned me about my boyfriend," Carol said bitterly.

Reggie's other friends changed the subject and ordered another round of wine. Reggie declined, knowing she had to be up early. She was already looking forward to her dinner with Sam.

She had never been in a relationship for more than one year, so there was that part of her that was waiting for "The One." She was not fast and loose, but she longed to be held by someone she loved and feel the passion she had felt a few times in her life. *Whoa*, she said to herself. *You haven't even gone out on the date, and already you're thinking about finding "The One."* She laughed and asked her friends to tell her all about their weeks and all the funny stories they had. She sat back, feeling content as the laughter and chatter continued.

Reggie was up early the next morning working on her stories. Most people didn't realize that her work involved gathering information as well as being a TV reporter. She wrote stories, did research, and made lots of calls. Her time on camera was not as frequent as some of the news people, but she loved her work.

She wanted to know more about the dead man and his connection to the explosion, if there was one. She dug in and started to do her research. Between her calls, she asked her boss what he thought of her going to the resort to do a follow-up on Maggie. She thought for sure he would say "No way," but he shook his curly hair and pushed his glasses up on his nose before saying, "Great idea, but I can't pay you for all your vacation expenses. How about you take vacation and I'll pay for a few nights and food?"

"Thanks, that would be great." she said, giving a thumbs up. She realized that wasn't very professional, but she had known him for a year, so he gave her his goofy grin and walked away from her desk.

She called Maggie. "I'm coming with you. Give me the details on the place and how to get reservations. Think my news status will get me in quicker?" she laughed.

She could hear the excitement in Maggie's voice and wrote down the directions and name of the place so she could make her reservations for a room. She had to remind herself that she was working, but there was something about getting out of town that made her smile all day.

***

What she did not know was that somewhere else in town, someone else was smiling. How convenient, he thought, after listening in on Maggie and Reggie's phone conversation. All the key players will be at the same resort. "You are making my job so much easier, ladies," he chuckled to himself. The parking lot was a mistake, and he prided himself on not making mistakes. He'd had a stolen car, avoided the cameras, and even had worn his blonde wig. It should have all gone well, but that bitch had to turn around at the last minute. She had ruined everything. He was tired of her ruining everything. He never goofed up…she was spoiling his record, and that made him livid.

CHAPTER 15

Reggie walked into the restaurant to meet Sam and did not see him anywhere. Suddenly he came through the door carrying a flower, and handed it to her. He said he hoped she did not think he was corny, but told her his mom believed that business or not, whenever he met a beautiful lady, he should take her a flower. The pink rose was actually Reggie's favorite color, and she found herself, like the time she first met him, staring into Sam's dark brown eyes. *He really is gorgeous,* she thought as the hostess escorted them to their table.

The dinner was laced with interesting conversation, some talk about the case, but mostly they ate and laughed a lot.

When it was time to leave, they walked out to the parking lot together and Sam leaned in so close to Reggie, she could feel his breath on her cheek. He put his arm around her waist gently and drew her whole body to him. Reggie turned her face up to his and felt her heart race as they kissed each other passionately.

Reggie's legs felt weak as she pulled away and said, breathing heavily, "I had a wonderful time, Sam."

"I did too, Reggie," Sam said, still holding her waist. "Can I see you again?"

"I would love that. I'm going to go with Mrs. Andrews for a story and a vacation, but when I get back, I would love to see you again."

Sam stepped back and said in a surprised voice, "Does Mike know you are going to go with Mrs. Andrews?"

"No. I haven't told him yet, but I don't need to ask his permission," she said, getting a little defensive.

"I know," Sam said. "I guess I'm still worried about the bomber, and your plans took me by surprise. Truth be told, I don't want you in any danger. I know I just met you, but I don't want you hurt either. Please tell Mike about this tomorrow, Reggie, or I feel I have to."

Reggie softened up as she realized that he was just concerned for her, not trying to tell her how to run her life. Or maybe he did not approve, but there was something about this man that made her want to see him again.

"Fine, I'll tell him tomorrow, but he's not going to talk me out of it."

Sam smiled. "I doubt that anyone could talk you out of something if you did not want them to."

"Ha, you're getting to know me already," Reggie chuckled.

"Call me when you get back, so we can see each other again, please."

"Will do," she said as she jumped into her Subaru and headed home. In her rearview mirror she saw Sam standing in the lot watching her drive off.

Good guy, she said to herself. *A good guy.*

The next day Reggie called Mike and filled him in on her

plans. There was dead silence on the other end.

"Are you out of your mind?" he sputtered. "It's too dangerous. I don't even want her to go."

"My boss says I can. I'm due for vacation, so it will be fun," Reggie said firmly.

"Do you realize how much danger you'd be in? We still haven't captured the bomber, and we think there is more of a connection with the dead guy, and you want to go on vacation with our only witness?" By now, Mike's voice was getting louder. "You can't go. I won't let you."

Reggie actually did not get angry. She just dug her heels in. "I'm going, and if you're so worried about us, why don't you come and protect us?"

"What, come there to protect you?" he said in disbelief.

"Sure, why not? You said you were concerned about her, and I've heard the tone of your voice when you talk about her. Not just another case is my belief, but if you came you could have a vacation like me, watch her, and as a matter of fact, watch me if this crazy person is around. Maggie likes you, and maybe you can stop them from getting hurt. Come to think of it," Reggie said, remembering what Maggie had told her, "I think she could be in danger." Reggie told Mike about the parking lot and that it was probably nothing, but there was something about it that made Reggie and Mike uncomfortable.

"Think about it, Mike. You would be doing your job, and the Feds might think you're Super Cop," Reggie said, this time really hoping to convince Mike to come.

Reggie did not know how Maggie would react, but there was something in Maggie's voice too when speaking of Mike that made her wonder if there was any chemistry there.

Reggie's lips still felt Sam's kiss from the night before, and she actually hoped the vacation went fast so she could have more of those kisses. She had been so focused on work that to feel the warmth of a man again was wonderful.

***

"I think it's a crazy idea, but I have to fill in my team on what is going on. You make sure you don't put yourself or her in danger. Are you taking your camera man?"

"No…this is a working vacation, Mike. I know you're worried, but really, I was not kidding. Think about coming. Hey, maybe I would feel safer too."

Mike was tempted. He knew that if he went he would have to keep in touch with his team for updates on the investigation. There had to be some connection to the man killed downtown.

"I have to go now. There's a team meeting with the ATF Agent and the FBI in ten minutes." Mike said a quick "Bye" and hung up the phone.

***

Reggie was tempted to call Maggie, but realized that she did not want to mention that Mike might come, because by his tone it sounded like a "no go." She had a lot of other stories to work on.

She and her assistant were looking over the man killed downtown and some more information on the businesses that were destroyed. *I'm a good reporter*, she thought, *and if anyone can find a connection, I can.*

CHAPTER 16

Mike shook his head as he walked into the meeting. He felt underdressed as he saw all the guys and ladies dressed in their blue suits, every hair in place. Mike looked down at his khaki pants, steel blue shirt, and policeman's tie. Not a slob, but certainly not a meticulous kind of guy.

Yet Mike was very detail-oriented in his cases, and often would see the link that others missed. There was something about this case that was upsetting Mike. Besides the fact that this was a professional job, why take out all the businesses if you just wanted revenge against one? Unless this was a case of misdirection. It amazed him that this guy was so good that there were no prints, but thanks to all the agencies' bombing experts, this guy must have a signature.

As Mike got himself a cup of coffee and sat down next to Lee Ann, one of the best detectives on his team, Agent Brian Whitaker started talking about their recent findings.

"Bad news, good news," Whitaker said. "The good news

is that we have found out more about the dead guy that ties him to this case. The bad news is we have a highly dangerous man on our hands. We were able to take the minute piece of the bomb your guy spotted and get a signature. Unfortunately, it's a guy that has been off our radar for a very long time. The last time he planted one of these things was in Minnesota ten years ago. There could have been more, but this is the one that we know of for sure. The people there were lucky. He planted it at a shop early in the morning like this one, obviously not wanting to hurt anyone, so there was no one injured in that bombing. There was one witness in that case, like this one, but she was killed hitting a tree in a car accident. Who knows, that could have been caused by our bomber a few weeks later. The report says that before her accident the witness gave pretty much the same description as this case…a man of average height with dark wavy hair. Never found a motive in that case, so we are looking at it again. We would not have found this one, but we ran your info through our databases and came up with this incident. We don't know if we have a terrorist, hit man for hire, or an insurance scam. Whoever this guy is he will not be found easily. No prints found in that case, either. He had gloves on, the witness said, but it was cold there so they did not think anything of it. Our witness in the first bombing had the car accident as she was headed to work. They didn't have the cameras they have now, but one did catch a glimpse of someone, showing a blond guy of average height with a goatee."

Mike's frown deepened. "Was anyone guarding the witness at that time?"

Brian sat forward, crossed his arms in front of him, and looked directly into Mike's eyes.

"No, they thought it was an isolated incident, and that

witness also didn't get a good look at the person. You were smart to put a detail on this witness."

Mike felt his stomach turn. "We have someone watching her house, but I found out today that she was almost run down in the grocery store parking lot. She dismissed it, but I'm worried. She's going on vacation for a week. She'll only be an hour away, and her sister and the reporter will be with her, but if this happened before it sounds like she could be a sitting target."

"We can't order her not to go, but she's a real target there if this person is still in the area. We're trying to pull the files for the surrounding areas. We may have to assign an agent to go to this resort to give protection to Mrs. Andrews. Do you have the manpower to cover this, Detective?"

"I could do it."

"That would be great," Whitaker said. "We can keep you posted from this end, and you can keep us updated. We don't want to cause any panic about this. It seems this guy only went after the witness, but who knows what he will do ten years later? What makes him dangerous is if he thinks she told us more than she did, or that she will suddenly remember something about him."

"Shouldn't we follow Mrs. Andrews everywhere, not just her home?"

"Good idea. Until she leaves, she is to have someone tailing her and her sister. No sense in taking chances."

"So you think this is retaliation against a business, and not some anarchist making a point?"

"What I think is that we have a very dangerous man out there that has done this before, and we don't know how many other times this has happened."

"Let's see if we can get the grocery store film for their

parking lot. I think they probably use the old film type and not digital, but we need to check on that. Maybe we can get a plate on the car that almost hit Maggie, if it was really planned." Mike suddenly realized he had made the right decision on going on the trip…maybe a lifesaving decision. Whitaker told him not to tell Maggie yet about the witness in the prior bombing. For now, the less she knew the better, but sooner or later she would find out the truth. If he told her she would laugh it off, but if he didn't she would be furious. All he knew now was that he had to tell her something sometime.

CHAPTER 17

Maggie and Alice loaded their suitcases into the car, waving to the car near the house, knowing it was the surveillance team. They had moved the car closer now that she knew she was being watched. Maggie had not heard any more from Detective Mike about the bomber, so she was eager to go to the hotel and have a grand time. She was glad Reggie was coming for a visit, and felt happy about that. She could almost feel the breeze that would caress her face as they took the ferry over to the island. The island was the most peaceful place she had ever been, and was only about ten miles around. The water around it was very cold, but she loved to feed the sea gulls, throwing crackers up in the air until they swooped down to grab them.

She was actually delighted that Mike was coming along to keep an eye on the "ladies." Many of Maggie's bruises had already turned yellow, and the pain she felt had mostly gone away. She was ready to swim, eat, drink, and laugh a lot. The island had little shops, carriage rides, wonderful food, and no cars, so they could enjoy a girls' shopping trip for one day. Her kids had called and said they were fine, so Maggie felt as if she was going on this trip a "free woman." Even Alice had that "Let's Party" look on her face.

Just as she shut the trunk, she heard a car pull in front of her house. Mike stepped out of his car.

"So, are you all ready to go?"

"Boy, are we," Maggie said as she walked to greet him halfway up the driveway. "You know, you can ride with us… we're not crazy drivers," she chuckled.

***

Mike had not planned on riding with Maggie, but it gave him the perfect opportunity to really keep close track of her and keep them safe.

"Sounds good to me, but I want to chip in for gas. It seems the price goes up every day."

Mike had not told Maggie more of the details about the bomber, and by the feeling in his stomach, he was starting to regret that, orders or not.

Mike loaded his suitcase in Maggie's trunk. Alice offered to sit in the back, but Mike said he was used to riding in the back seat. What she didn't know was that during the entire trip, while he would be talking or listening to their stories, his eyes and ears would be vigilant for anything that may happen along the way. He carried an ankle pistol that was easy to hide under his jeans and shirt. For this trip he had chosen to wear a nice long sleeved shirt and nice jeans, as the place they were going wasn't too fancy, but wasn't casual either. He had received approval to take some money from the department to pay for his portion and for the restaurant at night. Reggie's boss had allowed her to go as well and paid some of her expenses. Reggie herself did not know any more about the bomber, so while they were all together, she could also be in as much danger as Maggie, if this guy was still around. Hopefully the agent was wrong, and this guy was long gone from the area.

The ride in the car was fun, with Alice's love of music and Maggie singing along to the songs, and almost made him forget for a moment why he was on the job.

As they got closer to the boat, Mike told the ladies he was concerned that the bomber had not been caught, and he needed them to let him know if they were to take off and where they were going. He did not give them a lot of details, but did say he was still concerned about them, and that was part of the agreement, that they would accept his protection.

After they met up with Reggie there was a half hour ferry ride to the island. Mike frowned as he scanned the docks. He didn't know if this was such a good idea. The good thing was that they were contained on the island, and the bad thing was they were contained on the island. He hoped that he could protect Maggie, but maybe he should have brought a few of his guys along. He had informed the island police what was going on, out of respect.

Masses of tourists surrounded the docks. Mike and the others took one of the horse taxis up to the hotel. They turned the bend to see a massive old stone hotel set into the hills surrounded by gorgeous flowers, a horse barn, and a pool to the left of the hotel, with some guests riding horses around a ring. It looked like a picture out of a postcard to Mike.

He was aware that Maggie and her husband had come here for their honeymoon, and noticed sadness in her eyes. Anyone else may have missed that, but Mike knew what it felt like to have such memories. His wife's face quickly flashed before him, but as quickly as it did he pushed it out of his mind. He did not have the time to feel sentimental about his past, as his job was to protect. He had to stay focused.

"Does it look the same, Maggie?" he asked gently as they pulled around the circle in front of the entrance.

"Even better," Maggie said with a wistful voice. "When we were here, they didn't have the stables, and they've put in even more beautiful flowers."

Maggie did not seem to mind talking about her husband, and it even made her smile to remember some of the fun they had and funny things that happened on their honeymoon.

"I'm ready for lunch after that drive, and then how about a swim? Let me just text my boys that we've arrived safely."

"I want to text my husband too, Mike, and say we arrived safely," Alice said.

It was times like this Mike wished he had somebody to text about his safe arrival. His folks would know where he was in case of an emergency, and how they could reach him.

"Sounds great," they all chimed in at the same time as they headed for check-in.

***

Maggie did not expect to spend all her time with Mike, as she wanted girl time with Alice and Reggie, but his presence did make her feel safe. She was embarrassed to admit it to herself, but there was that feeling she'd felt about him before that made her feel like a school girl with that slight crush when meeting a new boy. It also embarrassed her that this was where the love of her life and she had honeymooned, and she was now feeling an attraction to someone else.

***

Mike had requested they all be on the same floor for safety reasons, and after checking in they had lunch outside at the restaurant and then headed back to their rooms to get changed to sit by the pool. Watching over the ladies while eating his lunch seemed like second nature to Mike, as he had been in charge of protecting many people throughout his career, and had learned how to read their body language.

He had not seen anyone suspicious at lunch and hoped the entire trip would be like that. He knew once Maggie learned more details about the case, that all would change.

Mike quickly changed and remained out in the hall until Maggie and Alice came out of the room. Maggie's hair was swept up on top of her head, showing the fading bruises on her neck. She looked so relaxed and happy when she started to giggle and said to Mike, "This is so cool, having our own bodyguard."

Mike's smile spread across his face as he said, "At your service, ladies."

"Aren't you going swimming, Mike?" Alice asked, seeing Mike in his shorts and top.

"Nope, but I would like to get some sun. Besides, how can I watch over you if I'm swimming?" he said, half-joking and half serious. What he didn't tell them was that it was easier for him to keep his gun in his holster on his shorts, with a top over it to cover the gun, instead of any swimsuit.

"Suit yourself, Detective Mike, but I guess we'll have to splash you a little to keep you cool in this sun," Maggie said as they found some lounge chairs that did not have full sun, but were not in the shade either. The pool area was surrounded by impatiens and manicured shrubs, and had a swim up bar. "I don't suppose you will join us for a drink later in the day, Detective," Maggie laughed, trying to imagine Mike swimming up to the bar in his shorts. Fortunately, there was one end of the bar you could reach by the cement around the pool.

"No, ladies. I may get some sun, but this is a working vacation," he said as he lowered himself into his lounge chair, making sure it had the best views to see all. He did not think this maniac would strike during the day with people around, but his last kill was so silent that he could not be sure.

Everything seemed peaceful as Maggie and her sister swam, Reggie read a book, and Mike kept scanning the crowd.

Suddenly there was a loud crash by the pool and Mike leaped up. He was just about to draw his gun when he realized it was just a waiter who had dropped a drink and the glass had splintered. Even Maggie froze in the pool and had that look of panic in her eyes. Her shoulders, which had stiffened moments before, relaxed as she saw that it was only a glass. She smiled at Mike, realizing he had jumped up to protect her, and mouthed the words "Thank you" to him.

Mike smiled back, but he felt uneasy again as he saw that there were many ways the maniac could get to her if he chose. If he was as good as they said, could Mike really protect her?

Mike sat in his chair, watching everyone and looking in all directions for anything unusual. He sighed as he realized it was going to be a really long week.

CHAPTER 18

They spent the next two days doing the same routine of breakfast, wandering, lunch, the pool, dinner, and a drink out on the veranda at night. All four of them developed a pattern of kidding each other, sharing food, and enjoying their time together.

On the third day the ladies wanted to shop in some stores that Mike did not even want to enter. They bugged him to let them go alone, but Mike insisted that he would give them space if they agreed he would be close by. Maggie found herself laughing more than she had in a long time, and besides her sister's zany company, Reggie and Mike were really fun to be with. She found herself staring at Mike more than she intended, especially when he laughed. His eyes would crinkle, and his laugh was a genuine belly laugh and sometimes a warm chuckle. Of course she learned more and more about him and Reggie too. If she had had a daughter, she would hope she would have been independent and sassy like Reggie. Reggie entertained them with reporter stories, Mike with his detective stories, and she and Alice fun stories from their lives. Mike seemed a little quieter than usual after dinner, and Maggie wondered if he had had just about enough of watching them. Instead of going into the pool with the ladies like Maggie had done the nights before, she stayed in her rocking chair near Mike. They chose the hotel's quiet side porch that overlooked the buoy's lights and the lights of other boats in the harbor down the hill.

They were the only guests on the porch, and the island sounds seemed to lull both of them into a peaceful relaxed state, but Mike's body showed a stiffness Maggie did not understand.

"Is everything okay, Mike?"

"I'm fine," Mike said unconvincingly as he looked into her eyes.

"Hey, you forget I'm almost a shrink," she laughed, touching his hand lightly.

It was as if an electrical current passed through their hands. The intensity of the touch seemed to startle both of them and they stood up at the same time, their bodies actually coming close together, and their eyes locked as they seemed to be memorizing each other's faces.

"Really, everything is okay," Mike said slowly, not wanting to move away from her body.

"I was just worried about you, Mr. Detective," she said, as she stayed close to him and looked into his eyes. She touched his shoulder and started to tell him she appreciated him protecting her, when he leaned towards her and hungrily kissed her lips.

Maggie knew she should have pulled away, but she leaned in and kissed him back, feeling his arm wrap around her waist and draw her close. After what seemed like an eternity, they pulled apart.

Mike started to sputter that he was sorry when she put her finger over his lips, and said, "I wanted to kiss you too. It does feel weird to kiss another man besides my husband, of course, but it also felt right. You're honest like he was, Mike," Maggie said softly.

Mike suddenly frowned and pulled away from Maggie. Maggie wondered what she had said for him to react that way. Maybe talking about her husband made him uncomfortable.

"Maggie, we need to go in now," he said, suddenly getting formal. "I loved the kiss, but I'm here on an assignment, and can't mix business with pleasure."

Maggie felt a little hurt by his reaction, but was not going to tell him that. In fact, she could have stayed on the porch and kissed him some more, but he was right. He was supposed to guard her, and here she was making his job harder. She didn't think she should tell her sister yet, but of course she would get it out of her, as only her sister could. Alice would probably say, "It's about time. Henry would want you to be happy, even if it was one kiss."

"Let's go in now, Maggie. You girls are doing your shopping tomorrow, and I have to get some sleep," Mike said, still sounding like a policemen on duty.

As he walked her to her door Maggie tried very hard to keep her distance, but she could feel the electricity in the air and longed to touch him.

Maggie walked into her room and leaned on the door as she shut it. *Oh, my God, I like that man*, she thought as she felt her body still tingling from their kiss.

Alice was sitting in her bed reading, but when she saw Maggie's face, she laughed and said, "Sit. Now tell me why you're glowing, as if I didn't know."

***

In his room, Mike put his gun on his nightstand and fell back onto the bed. *Boy, did I goof,* he thought. *I like Maggie, but for God's sake, I'm supposed to protect her, and I don't want her hurt because my feelings are getting in the way.*

Mike knew he was not supposed to reveal details to Maggie, but he felt guilty that he hadn't told her what had happened to the last person, or at least made her a little more cautious. Honest, she had called him. "Ha," he laughed bitterly.

Chapter 19

Breakfast on the porch had all of them laughing. Reggie felt that something was different, but couldn't put her finger on it. She was having a great time on this trip, and would occasionally interview Maggie for the piece she was doing. She felt like she was with her mom when she was with Maggie, but could even share more because she wasn't her mom. Maggie's sister Alice was a riot, too. Reggie had to check in on her other stories, and would leave time in the afternoon to actually get work done.

She got a text from Sam and felt her heart skip a beat. Something about that honeymoon period of dating made life seem all the more exciting.

After breakfast they headed to the downtown shops, with Mike close by as their guard. He had become a comfortable presence for them all, and was even willing to wait while they looked in every store today. Maggie thought this was unnecessary, as the man who blew up the stores was probably long gone, but she knew that was their agreement with Mike in order to go on the vacation.

The town was very busy with tourists crowding the streets and shops. Mike asked them to keep together, to all be in the same shop together, and to leave at the same time.

Mike waited by the door and told them to take their time. Reggie, Maggie, and Alice stayed only a few minutes in the souvenir shop, came out, and then went to the discount clothing store, telling Mike they would probably be there for a while. They tried on clothes and laughed as they put on hats and took a picture together. Alice bought a hat, but Reggie and Maggie just enjoyed having a "girl's" shopping trip.

They left the store and had started towards Mike, when suddenly a man ran in front of them with his arms outstretched, as if blocking them. Mike pulled his gun reflexively, and the women jumped back just as they heard a gunshot from some place away from the store. The man fell back on the porch as blood oozed down his chest. People started screaming and running from the store and down the street.

Mike yelled for the ladies to get to the back of the store, and they ran and hid behind the counter. Mike covered the door, and within five minutes the police from the town were at the scene and entered the store. Seeing Mike there they told him to drop his gun. Mike complied and loudly said, "I'm Detective Mike Pierce," he said, showing the police his badge. "I called your office here to say I would be on the island."

"You're a long way from home," one of the cops said. "You can come on the porch and tell us if you recognize this guy. Who are the ladies in the back?"

"They're with me. I'll explain outside." Mike told Maggie, Alice, and Reggie to wait in the store, and he filled the police in on a little of what was going on without telling them everything. The police asked Mike if he recognized the shooter as they carefully approached the individual. Mike's mouth dropped open as he recognized Al Case from his regional FBI office. Al Case was one of the agents Mike really respected, and he had a great wife and two kids. He leaned down and said, "It will be okay, Al. They're going to get you to the hospital…hang in there, buddy. What the hell are you doing here anyway?"

Al looked up into Mike's face before he passed out, and said weakly, "He's here, Mike. They sent me and one other agent to watch your back. Get her the hell away…let my guys handle this…just get her the hell away."

"He's one of us, officers; the real shooter is still loose on the island somewhere."

The officers quickly called in to their office and started the procedure for an island emergency.

Chapter 20

"Go, go," Mike said as he quickly got the women out of the store. "You're in danger, and we'll get your things sent later. We must go back now. The ferries will shut down for a while as they screen for security reasons, so we are all headed down that street, where a helicopter will be waiting for us." Just as he said that an FBI helicopter started to hover and land down the street. "Run," he said as he scanned the streets. Reggie forgot her fear for a moment and said she wanted to stay to cover the story. "Absolutely not," Mike said. "You're in danger now, too. You're coming with us. Police orders." Reggie started to protest but saw the hardness in his eyes, and started for the helicopter with Maggie and Alice.

As they ran to the helicopter door, a shot rang out and skimmed Alice's arm. An agent in the helicopter leaped from the chopper once it landed and headed towards the area they thought the shot had come from. The other person in the copter covered the girls and got Alice and the rest inside. Mike took a look at Alice's arm. Fortunately, it was just a grazing wound.

They were safely in the helicopter and were quickly going up before anyone said anything. Alice was pale, as were all of them, and Maggie, sitting next to her, was patting her arm to stem the flow of blood from her wound, telling her she would be fine.

"What the hell is going on, Mike?" Maggie said in a daze, but at the same time demanding answers.

"I knew I had to protect you, but I didn't realize just how much danger you really were in from this maniac."

"Maniac," Maggie said, her mouth dropping. "You knew this maniac may still be around and you didn't tell us? We have about a half an hour till we get wherever you're taking us, so start explaining...now." Maggie said, her eyes now flaming with anger.

Mike slowly explained to Maggie, Reggie, and Alice what really was happening. When he was done, he started to put his hand on her shoulder and she slapped it away.

"Don't you dare touch me. You lied to us. You got my sister hurt."

Mike looked at her, his face paling with shame and guilt, and said, "I didn't lie. I was doing as I was told, and trying to protect you."

Maggie shook her head and fumed. "It's wrong to keep the information from us. You could have gotten all of us killed."

"Would you have stayed at home and not gone on vacation if I had told you the truth?"

"Probably not, but that is not the point, Mike. You were not honest with me. I know you said you were ordered not to tell us, but I'm still furious. So where do we go from here, besides getting Alice's arm looked at?" Maggie said. "In fact, Alice, I want you to go home and get out of this mess. It's me this maniac wants, not you."

Mike said, "You're right. Alice, you need to get out of here for now, and I'm taking Maggie to a safe place."

"Like hell I will," Alice shot back at Mike. "I'm not leaving my sister."

"Alice, I would worry about you if you were here. Go back to your husband, be safe, and I'll survive. Mike, can you get her back without anyone knowing? What if this guy is part of your group? How did he know where we were going?" Maggie asked, looking more fearful at the thought.

Mike shook his head and rubbed his forehead. "I don't know how this guy found out, unless he's been following our every move. All I know is until we get him, you are in more serious danger than we thought, and you can't go home."

"What about my kids?" Maggie asked, obviously fearing the worst.

"You're going to stay away from them. Tell them whatever you need to without saying too much," Mike said seriously.

At that comment, Maggie's blood began to boil. "Screw that. I want my kids safe."

"This guy works alone as far as we know, and he is going to be wherever you are. We can request that someone watch your sons' apartments if you wish. Maggie, you have every right to be upset," Mike said, trying to make peace with her as the helicopter started its descent. "This guy didn't target the families, just the witnesses. It's you we need to protect, and you must tell your kids to stay away. I want to run a sweep of your home and make sure this guy has no access to you. You use a landline at home, so I want to check that, too," he said, feeling sick that Maggie and the others could have been hurt, and real bad that she was angry at him.

Reggie had been sitting quietly for once, her hands folded

in her lap to keep them from shaking. When it seemed that the storm of words was over between Mike and Maggie, Reggie said slowly and almost in a pleading voice, "You can stay with me, Maggie. I have a safe apartment, and I agree with Mike, it's too dangerous to stay at your home."

Maggie softened for a second and put her hand on Reggie's shoulder. "Thanks, Reggie, I would love to do that, but I'm worried about you going home. If he has been watching us this whole time he knows you are a friend, and may come looking for me at your place." Maggie couldn't stand the thought of another person getting hurt because of her, and she had grown fond of Reggie.

Reggie started to protest, but Mike said he thought it was a good idea as well. "You can still do your job, but stay as safe as you can."

"Mike, the minute I get back I have to do a story on this. You know reporters are starting to head up to the island as we speak to find out what went on. I promise I'll clear with you what I prepare, but I have to report something." Reggie turned to Maggie, feeling like a traitor that she was going to tell her story, but she knew she had to, and who better to tell it accurately than her. Reggie sounded brave, but inside she was in shock, as she had never been involved in a shooting first hand.

Maggie turned to her sister and talked to her in a low voice, so Mike could not hear. She turned back to Mike, her blouse sticking to her body from fear and sweat, and said in a firm voice, "Okay. Alice will go home and be safe, and I will go to a safe house or whatever you call it. I also want some sort of guarantee my boys will be safe. Reggie can come to the safe house with me for a while. I know you have to report on this, Reggie," Maggie said, seeing the look on Reggie's face, "but at least you will be away from your apartment. I will do whatever it takes to get this guy, and I will be damned if he is going to get me. And the last thing, Mike," she said, getting very close to his face so he could hear exactly what she was saying in a voice hard like steel. "No more secrets. If you know something, you tell me. Is it a deal?"

Mike started to open his mouth, but instead raised his right hand.

"Deal."

***

The helicopter landed, and back on the island, the bomber stood on the ferry deck pretending to wave at someone on the dock. It didn't matter that he had to throw away his clothes and change his wig, and after the botched attempt to kill Maggie, toss his gun away as well. There would always be another gun, and other chances.

He hid his clenched fist in his pocket, the same fist that he would have liked to use to slam into that stupid detective's face. He must keep reminding himself why he blew up that damn computer shop in the first place. All that work the bomber did to make it hard to tell what business was targeted.

The end would certainly be worth all this aggravation. Another miss…his boss was going to be mad as hell, like he was. Wrong place, wrong time. You're dead…you're mine.

CHAPTER 21

Maggie and the rest were quickly helped down from the helicopter and into a black SUV, which was waiting for them. It took them to Maggie's house and stood guard as Maggie was told to get her things together and Alice packed to go home. They were instructed not to say a word in the house, because Mike and the FBI were still not sure if there was a bug somewhere that they had missed. As they roamed the house, both Alice and Maggie became teary eyed as they realized how serious this all was, and that maniac would not just "go away." Alice and Maggie filled the silence of the house by stopping every few minutes or so to exchange a sisterly glance or give each other a quick hug.

With Mike's help they both finished packing, quickly threw out anything that needed to be thrown out in the fridge, gathered her box of bills and important papers, and Maggie turned on the lights she wanted to stay on. The unreal part to all this was that it was like they were going on vacation again and getting the house in order…except this time she felt sick to her stomach at what had happened. She was glad her cat was with her friend, but she would miss her.

As their things were put in two separate cars, Maggie held Alice close and, getting teary eyed again, said, "Alice, I'm so sorry to have gotten you into all this. I would be lost if anything were to happen to you. Be safe, I love you. I'll call you tonight."

Alice hugged Maggie and, as she got into the car, turned to Maggie and said, "Without any hesitation, I can say this was the most action packed visit I've ever had with you."

Maggie started laughing and said, "Only you could say that." enjoying the last "sister" moment they would have for a while, each knowing how frightened the other was.

Reggie was in Maggie's car's backseat making a few calls to the news desk when Maggie got in the car.

Mike jumped in the front seat and turned back to Maggie and Reggie, wincing a little from moving too fast and feeling a sudden pull in his shoulder.

"Maggie, we'll give you a special phone, and one to your sister as well. They will be secured so you can talk to each other. We're also checking your place and home phone for any bugs. We still don't know how he found out about the island trip. He may have been following us. They say this guy is a master at blending in, so he could have been anyone. The FBI is checking footage of the island."

***

Maggie chose to be silent on the way to Reggie's, and offered to help her with carrying anything from her apartment. Instead, Reggie took in Mike to help her get her things quickly.

Once inside and throwing things in a huge suitcase and her valuables in a huge box, she turned to Mike and said, with

112

hands on her hips, "Boy, are you in trouble. You really blew it with Maggie…you almost got her killed. I know you like her, so Detective Mike, you're going to have to get this maniac and keep us informed. Now tell me as I pack what I can't say for my story."

Mike sighed, and began his instructions.

***

Everything was in the car and they headed to what looked like any apartment, anywhere in the suburbs. Nondescript, looked like all the others, brick, nice black shutters, two stories tall.

But this was different, Mike said as he pointed out the cameras at the front door, and when they got inside he went over the safety features in the apartment.

"There are three bedrooms, ladies, one for each of you and one for the FBI agents that will be assigned to you. There is an alarm system and a panic button. We have constructed a fake wall that leads into a small closet. If all else fails you have a place to hide." Mike pointed out the bookshelves disguising a hidden door like one would see in the movies, but it was done so well that no one would know it was actually a bookcase fake door.

"I'll be stopping by daily, and you will be accompanied by an FBI agent when outside the apartment for any reason. You will not call your friends, except your neighbors with the special phone to tell them you are continuing on vacation, and to give instructions for your cat. You can call your family once or twice a week on the throwaway phones and assure them you're safe.

"You will not tell anyone where you are. If you need something, we'll get it for you. If you're bored, we have shelves of books in here, and wonderful televisions and movies to watch. Reggie, you are going to be the 'problem.' For a while, going to the station is out. If this guy can follow us to the island, he can follow you here. You can call in your story, but no live TV."

Reggie looked at Mike with a shocked expression. "No on-air story? That's not fair."

"It's better to be safe than another victim of our bomber. Agent Case is recovering, but it could have been Maggie or you."

Maggie couldn't resist. As she sat on the couch, she turned to Mike and said, "Maybe we wouldn't have had anyone hurt if you had kept us informed." Sarcasm dripped from her mouth.

The minute she said it, even though she was furious at Mike, seeing the hurt and sheepish look on his face made her want to take back her cutting words.

"I'm mad, Mike, but I realize you were only trying to protect us. Now let Reggie and I become involved in trying to help find out why this killer wanted to blow up the store. I spend my life trying to help people figure things out. I'm not a policeman, but maybe we can use this time to help find out who this killer is. I'm worried that word will leak out about where we are. Who knows we're here?"

"My boss, the FBI, and Alice. I have instructed the FBI agents to check for any leaks, and they are looking to see what calls were placed from our department's cell phones."

Just as Mike was about to touch Maggie's shoulder to reassure her, his cell phone rang.

"Detective Pierce." He listened intently, his deep blue eyes clouding over a little. "Thanks for letting me know." He turned to Maggie. "Not good news. Looks like our guy tapped into your landline. We'll be watching your home through our digital cameras, and have taken care of the outside wires. We have a guy from our division parked outside your house, keeping an eye on the telephone poles."

"Now how about we start looking at your evidence and making some headway," Maggie said firmly. "I'm not about to sit here reading and watching television. If this guy is going to come after me, I want to be ready. I want to know what he really looks like, and why he blew up the building," Maggie said, beginning to feel in control for the first time in a long while.

***

Mike stood up from the couch, his shoulder still aching, and said, "Okay. I'll have Sam bring the files over in an unmarked car and we can get to work. The refrigerator is stocked so we can eat here. I'm so sorry, Maggie, for not telling you more. They said I shouldn't, but I should have," Mike said, really hoping Maggie would forgive him.

For the first time since the night on the porch, Maggie softened towards Mike, and she laughed. "So we are going to have some good home cooking, I hope."

"As a matter of fact," Mike chuckled, "I'm a damn good cook, so we won't go hungry."

Mike made his call to his division boss on the secured line, again telling him to keep this to himself and the person he would send over with the files.

"Okay, ladies, files will be over within two hours."

Next he called the FBI and asked them to have the agent give him a call on his cell and give him an update on what they had found.

Reggie got on the computer and typed up her story. They let her put in most of the information, but kept out the part about Maggie's phone line being bugged, anything about

Maggie's family, and that it was the computer store that was targeted. Mike and the team had Reggie put in that Maggie had been relocated to another town to throw the killer off track.

The files arrived and they started poring through them. Mike had found out that the computer store had a backup unit at a separate location, but if they knew that, then the bomber probably did too. They sorted through the files to see what connection this bombing might have to the one ten years ago, and any clue to who the bomber was. They found out that ten years earlier the business that was bombed belonged to a local business owner in Minnesota. There were no prints at the scene, and the police had no idea that the witness would be in danger until she came up dead from the car accident. They had used the footage from around the location of the car accident—stores, restaurants, and traffic cams—but since the cameras were even less sophisticated then than now, except one grainy image of a man with a book bag, there was nothing. They couldn't even be sure that the man in the image was the killer, but since they had placed him near the scene of the bombing, again only from that grainy picture, he may just be the guy. Or he could be a local resident who just happened to be in town at the time.

Mike handed the picture to Maggie. "Think this is the guy you saw?"

Maggie took the picture, put on her glasses, and kept looking at the photo.

"Could be," she said slowly. "There's something in his cocky smile that makes me think this could be the guy. Can't see his eyes, but he has the same 'All you police are morons' smirk. Why do they think the business was bombed ten years ago?"

"The police said the owner of the business was a local who had been suspected by the officials of selling and trading endangered animals on the black market. This is a big business world-wide. They were just about to nail him when the explosion happened. They thought it might be that someone was getting nervous about their animal ring being found out, and hired our guy to snuff him out. The poor woman who was our witness didn't expect to take a walk one day, see this guy near that guy's car, and be in extreme danger."

"Like me," Maggie said softly, looking into Mike eyes.

"The only difference is, we are going to get this guy and you will not end up dead." Mike said, his jaw hardening.

"You're right. We will get him, so let's keep going," Maggie said, her voice strong this time as she started through the files.

Maggie did not know a lot about facial recognition, but she wondered if they put this photo in the system and tried to compare it to any photos of anyone local, if there would be a match in their database.

"The FBI is running it now with the local database and state database. He looks to be about forty-five, fit, Caucasian, handsome, but who knows for sure? This guy wears disguises and uniforms…that's how he became a lineman. We are getting a new laser fingerprint machine in a few weeks, so that may help in finding a match."

Reggie stood up and started pacing the room. "Have you checked the hotel footage around town? Maybe this guy is staying somewhere local, and you could find out if they have seen anyone out of the ordinary. Could you show his picture around?"

"The FBI and ATF already have some of their people on it. As far as we know, this guy has been laying low for ten years, so we don't even know if he could be your local stock trader working in an office, and all the people around him think he's Mr. Nice Guy."

***

Mike suddenly remembered the break-in and the dead guy downtown and told Maggie about it. Reggie knew about the man of course, but she had not heard an update.

"Oh, my God, Mike," Maggie said, her excitement growing. "That may be our clue. Did they search the dead guy's house and look for fingerprints?"

"Yes, they did. In fact, this guy who broke in helped himself to a soda and left it on the table, but there were no prints on it, and no glass used or paper cup thrown away. This guy is careful and no fool, but I think we need to go over to that house and learn more about the dead guy to see if there are any connections to this case or the one ten years ago. I'm going to send Sam over to see if they can find anything else."

Reggie turned to Mike and said, "Hey, don't put Sam in danger, too."

"I can't promise any of us won't be in danger," Mike protested. "But Sam's careful, and if anyone can find a print, he's our guy. Besides, anyone guarding you becomes a target. I'm sure we are making this guy very nervous now, and if he is working for someone they must not be too happy about Maggie being alive or us looking so closely into this case. When they made a bomb and shot an agent, they made it personal with a lot of us in law enforcement."

"So let's get back to work," Maggie said, putting a new stack of files on her desk. "Please fill me in on this animal trade you're talking about."

"Yes, boss," Mike teased, glad that she didn't hate him at the moment. There was something about her being near him. He wanted to take her in his arms and give her a long, lingering kiss, feeling her warm body pressed up against his. He was almost embarrassed at feeling himself respond to her being this close, but her light scent of vanilla perfume made him desire her. This was the first time he had really desired anyone since his wife's death. He had been with a woman or two, but this was different, very different.

He also carried a new fear that he had almost gotten her killed, and he felt responsible for keeping her safe. And that scared the hell out of him.

CHAPTER 22

While dinner was cooking, Mike educated Reggie and Maggie about the illegal animal trade. Reggie was just setting the table and ready to take a break from the files when the doorbell rang. She instantly tensed up and stood in place by the table. Mike and Maggie froze in the kitchen. Mike silently motioned for Maggie and Reggie to get to the back room. He looked up at the screen of the door monitor and his body instantly relaxed. He opened the door and Sam came in, frowning.

"It's Sam, ladies. Come on out," Mike yelled.

Maggie and Reggie came out, each holding a fireplace poker for protection.

Sam held up his arms and laughed. "Please don't hurt me. I guess you ladies won't go down without a fight."

Sam pulled up a chair and sat down at the table. His smile vanished and his face became deadly serious. "I had to do all sorts of maneuvering to get here. I even used two cars, and no one at the office knows. I just don't trust this guy not to try to find the source of your news story. I spent at least two hours at this dead guy's home, and no prints. Nothing. This guy's too good. But," he said, as he cracked a small smile, "I did find a well-hidden file in our dead guy's bedroom. I used to think it was only in the movies that people taped things under a drawer, but bingo, this guy did just that. Our mastermind missed this. Maggie must have thrown him off his game a little, which is probably rare for this guy."

"So what was in it?" all three of them asked.

"There was just an invoice for a local finance company. I don't know how that ties in, but now we know for sure that this guy had business dealings with this finance company. They have a local branch here, and they do business with the firm this man worked for," Sam said.

"Was there anything else in the file?"

"Yes, two things. There was a piece of paper with a local phone number on it, and the other was a receipt. Get this," Sam said. "It was a work slip for the computer store that was bombed. Apparently, he left his computer there two days before the bombing. It looks like something was on that computer that our killer did not want anyone to find. I'm not sure why this guy would drop off a computer with sensitive information on it."

"What about the phone number?" Maggie asked.

"Well, I tried running it through our files, but believe it or not I came up with nothing. Even tried the phone company, and they don't have a listing for it."

"Did you try calling it?" Reggie asked, her reporter mind taking over.

"No, I wanted to check with Mike and make sure of our next move. I brought a throw away phone. Want me to try it now, Mike?"

"Go for it," Mike said. "Hush up, everyone."

Sam dialed the number. They waited and waited until Sam said, "Hello, is Sid there?" He listened for a second, and said with apologetic voice, "Sorry pal, I'm trying to reach this guy and he gave me this number. What city am I calling? Oh, I'm sorry, I must have dialed wrong...sorry." He hung up, and then gave them a thumbs up while smiling.

Reggie and Maggie both jumped up at the same time and said, "Tell us."

Sam said, "It was a guy on the phone, and he was not happy to get a call. It was obvious that he expected someone else. He said I had reached the finance company we are looking into, the same one that we found on the slip of paper in the dead guy's apartment. And as I said, they are the same ones who paid our dead guy's pay checks. When I asked what city he was in, he said this one, but I did not want to push it any further. We will probably receive a call back to see who we really are."

"I need to tell our regional special agent with the U.S. Fish and Wildlife Service about this, or have the FBI contact them. They can run a background check on this business. If these are our animal smugglers, they will probably obtain a warrant and get the files. We have so many agencies involved that it is good we all work well together. Plus, you don't shoot an FBI agent without repercussions," Mike said.

Mike shook his head before continuing. "I'm trying to figure something out regarding this. If this group is smuggling animals and the dead guy put it on his computer, then took it to a shop, I wonder if he thought he should store the computer somewhere else, for insurance, like the hidden envelope. Or maybe it was broken, and he was dumb enough to take it in.

It will be interesting to see if there were backup files and who they listed as the contact number for the computer. If this guy really thought he was in danger and wanted to get the computer out of his house, he would have probably given someone else's name for the pickup that he trusted, not our corporation....

"Sam, why don't you go downtown and get this all started? I still worry we have a mole somewhere, so it is mandatory that no one email, phone, or mention that Maggie, Reggie, or I are here. This guy is smart enough to find out our location, maybe through news stories about Maggie, whether she is gone or not. He's just too smart...or should I say, THEY — whoever they are — are just too smart."

"Will do," Sam said as he gathered his things. "And by the way, that was a fantastic dinner. Can I get assigned to stay here too?" He laughed, looking directly at Reggie. "Will you walk me to the door, Ms. News Lady?"

"Sure," Reggie said. As she walked him to the door, Maggie and Mike exchanged a knowing smile and started taking the dishes out to the kitchen.

***

As they got to the door, Sam stood very close to Reggie, touching her hand lightly. "I haven't forgotten we're due for another date."

Reggie looked up into his eyes and said, "I haven't forgotten either."

Sam gave her the softest, quickest, and most tender kiss on her lips, smiled, and headed out the door. Reggie gave a lopsided grin and a final wave, saying, "Please be careful." as she watched him quickly walk away.

***

In the kitchen Mike and Maggie started dividing up the

duty of cleaning up with a rhythm, as if they had been doing this as a couple for years. Reggie said goodnight and headed for her room.

When they were all done, Mike started to leave the kitchen, saying good night to Maggie just as she was headed thru the door. They lightly bumped into each other and Mike touched her arm. Their eyes met, and Maggie could see Mike struggling not to grab her and kiss her. She started to say something but he pulled away, his eyes still locked on hers, and said gently, "Goodnight, Maggie. See you tomorrow."

"See you tomorrow, Mike."

Maggie started to leave when she suddenly turned to him and gently touched his face.

"I'm not mad at you anymore, Mike," she said, keeping her hand on his cheek. "Goodnight."

Pulling her hand away slowly she headed towards her bedroom, wanting to turn around and run to him and feel the warmth of his arms. She stopped herself, as she knew she had to direct all her energy to getting this man who could kill her and ruin the life of everyone she loved. But she couldn't stop the feelings that were erupting for him.

I'm sorry, Henry, she said into her pillow that night. *There will never, ever be another you, never a love like you and I had. But for the first time I have this ease with someone like I had with you…. Please don't be mad….* Her eyes were teary as she drifted to sleep peacefully. For the first time in days, she felt safe with Mike nearby.

***

Somewhere in the city, the dark haired man was trying to explain to his boss why all went wrong on the island, and why he could not find the location of the woman. She had to come back to her house sometime, and when she did, she would wish she hadn't.

He had spent years hiding his occupation in this crappy city. But the good part was his getting to travel around, being able to do other jobs that needed his skills. He prided himself that he never hurt innocent people, women or children, and never would. Ten years ago he'd had to take care of the witness who could have gotten him caught. This time, once again, a woman had seen him. For the second time in his career he had made a mistake…in fact, a few mistakes. He could not tolerate mistakes, and his employer certainly wouldn't.

He sipped a cognac, kissed his already asleep wife gently, and turned the light out to sleep. He would have to keep his stamina up, and then tomorrow find Maggie. He must be rested. There were and would be many nights he would live in the shadows, and not have the luxury of sleep. With years in this city, it was amazing that only the ONE at the company knew of his existence. The traitor who was about to expose everything had been the only other one who knew about him, but he had been eliminated. With the thought of that successful elimination, he peacefully fell into a deep sleep.

CHAPTER 23

Reggie was lucky to catch Mike in the kitchen before Maggie awoke. She didn't mind hiding out for a while, but she was a reporter, for God's sake, and she had a job to do.

As Mike was making eggs at the stove, she asked, "Mike, how about if I stay at my apartment, and if I have to go in to work, one of your people could escort me? I wouldn't come back here, so no one would know about Maggie and this place. I can help you by using some of our databases at work to learn more about the animal smuggling into the United States. I really can tell you more if I stay at my place and go to work. Is that okay?"

Mike turned back to the eggs, and without saying a word put the eggs on a plate, slathered two pieces of toast with butter, and set down two cups of coffee. He motioned for Reggie to sit down. She said "Thanks, Mike," a little confused that Mike was not answering her question.

Mike took a few bites of his meal and looked Reggie in the

eyes. "I know this is not easy for you, and I know you want to help us. We can take you from here to work, but I'm asking you to just give us two weeks, and I promise that you will get the exclusive on this story. Maybe you could find out some information on the company, but I need you to work with us on the other info we get as we check them out. We think we have a problem with our shooter, but we don't know how many more of these guys there are at the company. It is bad enough to have one person trying to get to Maggie and you, but because you can lead them to her, you could get killed. What if there is more than one assassin?" he said, with a strong emphasis on the word "Killed." "Maggie really needs you to be here now. At least the two of you are in this together, and you both may come up with something. There will be times I have to leave, and I don't feel comfortable leaving either of you alone, even with one of the detectives. I promise we are not leaking anything to other reporters about the animal trade, since that would blow the whole deal. All those involved would start scattering, and our assassin would really be long gone. That might be good for now, but we don't know who else would come after you, or if he would be back to finish the job. We have to get this guy, and his boss or bosses, so you guys can live your lives again," Mike said.

***

Maggie came into the room, showered and dressed, her hair still wet and starting to curl around her face. She headed to the kitchen after saying hello to finish off the pan of scrambled eggs. She got her plate, thinking it had been a few months since she had someone join her at the breakfast table.

She used to get up with her husband to have coffee and read the paper, and still missed the conversation back and forth as they found ways to solve the world's problems. Now she felt a pang of sadness, missing life with Henry, so this morning she was glad she could sit at the table with Reggie and Mike. She sat down, but looking at the serious looks on both Mike's and Reggie's faces, felt her own mood darken.

"Okay, what's up, you two?" she asked.

Mike smiled and said, "Darn, I forgot you were a social worker. Can't get away with anything, can we?"

Reggie sipped her coffee. "I wanted to go back home and back to work, but Mike has assured me that's not such a hot idea."

"I bet Mike promised you could have an exclusive if you hung in there, right?"

Reggie could not help laughing. "He did, and it worked. I want an exclusive, but I really do want to help you crack this case, and I don't want to put anyone in danger. I have to be able to tell my parents something, because if they really knew all that was going on they would jump in their car and come here, vowing to drag me up to their home to keep me safe."

Maggie smiled. "We parents protect our babies, even if they're thirty years old."

"What if these guys go after my parents? I have to tell them something." Reggie felt her chest tighten with worry.

"These guys won't go after your parents," Mike said, "but I would tell them you're working on an undercover story, and if anyone asks them where you are, they can honestly say that they don't know. I don't think it will come to that. Besides, if anyone calls for you, tell your folks to let you know and we can trace the call. You can call some of your colleagues or friends with the burner phone and say you're working on an undercover story and won't be seeing them for a while. Keep it short and simple. Get your boss to drop any further mention of the story, and promise him you'll get an exclusive when it's all over."

Maggie understood how Reggie felt, and worried that her own sons could be in danger. She had told them their only contact should be with the throwaway, and to notify Mike on his phone if anyone strange asked about her. She was glad they lived far away, and hoped Mike was right, that the killer's only concern was finding her in this city. For some reason she knew she should be worried for herself, but she wasn't.

"Let's get to work looking at the files and see what we can find. Was there any word from the FBI?"

"We asked them to put someone in the company. We don't want to scare off anyone, but if there is a smuggling ring it could lead us to the killer. Maybe we could find out what information was so secret that they would blow up a computer business, kill a man, and follow you to the island."

"Who is this person?"

"We have to keep that top secret. We don't want any leaks. This person will get back to the FBI director and me through my track phone. They'll be sweeping my office and the rest of the department for bugs."

"Sounds good," Maggie said as she went to the living room and started to pore over the files with Reggie and Mike.

After several hours, Maggie asked Mike if they had any webcams in the area. She had never looked up webcams in her city, but when she had wanted to go to New Orleans or other cities, she had used them to get a sense of the city. It was as if she was "right there."

"There are some sites that locals run. We are not a big city, but we do have lots of residents who love to film things in the city, and have permission to set up a webcam for all to see. Let me check with the city and see who has permits. I also bet there are many that are up and running that we can find on the Internet that people put up without licenses. Good idea, Maggie. Our killer may have been taped, or there may be cameras close to the business that are 'live feeds.'"

CHAPTER 24

Mike got off the phone with a big smile on his face and an upbeat voice. "Bingo. We have a local who has some feed from a webcam near our dead guy's kill spot. I'm heading over there now to see what we can find out. Sharon will keep an eye on you ladies." Maggie and Reggie had gotten used to Mike calling them "The Ladies," but Maggie still smiled when he referred to them as that. There was just something cute about it.

***

Mike headed over to the house about ten minutes away and knocked on the door. He expected to see a man answer it, but instead a redhead in her late twenties answered it, keeping the screen door locked between them.

"Good morning, ma'am. Is this the Tucci residence?" Mike asked.

"What if it is?"

"I'm Detective Pierce. I was wondering if I could talk to

you about your webcam, Mrs. Tucci."

"It's Miss Tucci, Detective. I didn't do anything illegal. My website's on the up and up. I have a friend who owns the store it's set up in. A lot of the relatives of the townspeople like to see it to remember the town, and also see what kind of weather we are having. For me, it's just fun."

"I'm not here to arrest you, Miss Tucci. I just need to see some feed stored in your computer for a case we're working on."

"Show me your badge and I might let you in." Then she smiled and winked. "And I might let you call me Bobbi." She read Mike's badge carefully through the screen door, then stepped onto the porch, glancing around to see if it was just the two of them. "So, what's this case you need my footage for?"

"There was a murder downtown, and we think that your webcam could have captured some film of the killer."

***

Bobbi pursed her lips as she mulled over if she really wanted to help with this, and did she really want to let this cop inside her home. He looked decent enough, but didn't all sociopaths, she laughed to herself. Finally, she stepped aside and directed him to come in. She led him to her main room where she kept her computer, and gently shooed her cats away.

***

Bobbi sat down at the computer and turned to Mike. "What date do you want me to show you?"

Mike read from his notebook the date and time he needed. The woman found the footage and played it for Mike, speeding through it until she had a few people in her sights, and then slowing it down so Mike could look. They sat there for a long time when all of a sudden he saw a blond man suddenly slump down to the pavement. "Stop. That's him. That's the guy I'm looking for. Now can you scan the area and see if there's anyone near him…a car, or anything?" Mike said hopefully.

Bobbi smiled. "You bet. Not to brag, but when I set this up, I wanted to let people see all different angles and be able to zoom on to a certain area as needed."

She moved the camera around a little and Mike said, "That's it."

There on the camera was a car across from the dead man that matched the one seen right before the bombing. Inside the car you could see the shadowy outline of a person holding something that might be a gun, but Mike couldn't tell.

"Can you get the license plates?"

Bobbi tried, but they could not see them. She followed the car on her webcam as long as it would let her. They couldn't make out a license plate, but at one point there was a good side profile of a face and what looked like a gun.

"Thanks. You've been a big help," Mike said. "Can you send me this feed?"

"Sure. Where do you want it sent to?"

"Send it to my computer. No, wait. That may not be safe. Send it to this e-mail." Mike turned as he headed for the door. "Thanks, Miss Tucci. Can we contact you about other cases in the future?"

"You can call me Bobbi," she grinned. "Call any time. I'd love to be of assistance."

Mike left, eager to show the image to his FBI contacts and see if their facial recognition programs could ID this guy. He headed back to the apartment, calling Jim along the way to see his progress in trying to get inside the financial business.

"It's a stall," Jim said. "They need someone to work as an analyst, so I'll be going undercover. Everything's in order and I'm ready to go in tomorrow, but for some reason I'm being stalled. I won't be able to contact you for a while, so you and the ladies keep safe. If anything changes you know how to reach me."

Mike had a bad feeling about Jim going in, and worse about this being stalled, but Jim insisted. And besides, he was one of the best undercover agents available.

No one in this city knew Jim, so his cover would be safe. Mike didn't even know where he was staying, and it was always best to keep it that way. Yet, something still bothered Mike that he couldn't put his finger on…something bothered him a lot, and worried him a lot about this company.

Mike headed back to the apartment, using his usual many paths to get there. For the first time he felt unnerved as he realized if he could find out where Bobbi lived, the bomber could find her, too. He felt himself dripping with nervous sweat for the first time in a long time.

***

Maggie looked through the files with Reggie. The financial company consulted with companies and the government, and the employees had to have major security clearances. They seemed to have employees all over the world. The office in their city was one of the smallest, and most of the employees were on a consultant schedule, working out of town during the week and returning to work out of their homes on Fridays. The regional CEO of the company whose office was local seemed like an honest and good person, one of the few CEOs of a company that was female. That was changing in the United States, but not fast enough, Maggie thought.

The CEO who headed this office had worked her way

up from a business analyst, and often gave speeches at community gatherings about business and economics. She had been married, but due to her work schedule joined the ranks of the "divorced because of working and traveling too much." She lived on the far side of town in a swank condo with security, and had a driver take her back and forth to work. You didn't see people being carted around that much, if at all, in this small town. Her neighbors described her as "Nice," "Serious," or "Seemed Smart" when they were asked when she re-applied for her security clearance.

She had been born and raised in town, but had extensively traveled before her job to South America and Africa as the daughter of two missionaries. She said she felt it was her duty to help others. When the government looked into the places she had been to and how she'd helped, she received "glowing recommendations." She passed security clearances, lie detector tests, and drug tests to become the head of the office and regional head of the company. Being regional head meant she had to travel to various offices to see how the teams were doing.

Maggie thought, *Sounds too good, or maybe I'm being paranoid.* But she traveled to Africa and South America, and she would have access to various connections around the world for animals. Maggie could not wait till the FBI agent went in to see if he could get any more information. Here she was a social worker, always obeyed the law, and she was rooting for an agent to get information secretly from a citizen that might lead to the monster trying to kill her.

***

At the same time, Reggie was going over all the files that pertained to the killing of the woman ten years ago. Wrong place, wrong time…he got her so quickly. The grainy picture made Reggie think of something, but she could not put her finger on it. He looked so familiar…but from where?

She had done extensive traveling with girlfriends and watched news stations almost obsessively, so she probably had seen someone that looked like this man. She rubbed her forehead as she did when stressed, trying to blend everything together. But he did look familiar.

Reggie called her folks and her boss to let them know she was okay. She told her boss that she really was gathering a lot of stuff on the story. Then, her mind drifted to Sam, and she was hoping he would stop by with more information on the case.

"Thinking of Sam?" Maggie smiled.

"Was it that obvious?"

"You have every right to think of him. He's a 'hunk,' and I think he likes you, too. Life is too short not to tell the ones we want that we like them…so go for it." Maggie said.

"You mean like you telling Mike that you like him," Reggie teased.

Maggie's face flushed. "Do as I say, not do as I do. I like him, but this is new for me. I will always love Henry, and Mike pisses me off sometimes, but there is something good and honest about him, like I felt about Henry. I can't help but feel that Henry might say, 'Go for it' too."

"What about your sons?"

"They miss their dad, but I think they would be happy if I found someone. Not to replace him, but just to have someone to laugh with and be with, like I did with their dad. I don't think I ever want to marry again, but it would be nice to have someone in my life to fall in love with and be a companion through life's adventures, or just to sit and eat popcorn and have a beer with. I'm independent like you, Reggie, and have friends. No one would ever be the 'love of my life' like Henry, but it would be nice to have a companion again."

Maggie felt herself turn beet red when she realized she had only known Mike for a month and she was talking like this. *Wow, slow down*, she told herself. "Have you ever been in love, Reggie?"

"Once, and I really thought we would get married. But after one year, he dumped me. He needed to find himself, he said. I was pretty crushed, so I've avoided getting involved, I mean really involved, with anyone. But then Sam kissed me after our date, and I don't know… it felt good. Of course, I'm still relationship shy, and the next person I fall in love with will have to jump through hoops to get me to say I love him, but I don't know, maybe I'm ready again."

"Good luck to both of us then," Maggie said softly.

"Amen," Reggie smiled as she picked up her notes.

They spent the rest of the time looking at pictures of possible suspects in the files. They looked at the company, hoping to find out why someone would want to blow it up. Reggie kept wondering why the bomber waited ten years to do it again. If this guy was such a psycho, why wait ten years? *Maybe he didn't*, she suddenly thought. Maybe he had killed and bombed before, but the police did not know it. What if he had killed, but not bombed, before, and that was why he went undetected for all these years. The country was full of murders.

"Maggie, what if this guy has killed before? Maybe Mike can get his hands on cases that are similar to this killing. Maybe this guy gets around a lot more than we know. I wish I could go into that company and help the agent find out what's going on. I'm getting cabin fever. Let's ask Connie if we can at least go out back and get some sun. Connie," Reggie called out, "we're going to be out back on the patio. Do we need you out there?"

Connie came walking into the room from watching the television monitor. She was short, wore her hair in a security bun style, and seemed to check out everything in all directions wherever she went. She smiled at Maggie and Reggie, knowing they must be feeling cooped up, and said, "You can go out on the porch for about ten minutes, but be careful and wear hats to cover your faces, because we do not know about this guy."

Maggie and Reggie went outside, and Maggie told Reggie she was surprised by Connie's comments. How could this guy find them? Reggie shrugged and said it was better to be careful. They soaked up the sun and talked about a lot of things in their lives. Mike had assured them that the two townhomes on each side were rented by them, so there would be no way for people to overhear what they were saying, but they felt they needed to be careful. Each of them felt energized by getting outside, and awaited Mike's return to hear if he had learned anything.

***

In another part of town, the bomber was getting closer to finding out where the women were. Did they think he was an idiot and that he would not be able to find them? Little did they know about him, and they underestimated his intelligence. Everyone always underestimated his intelligence, and that was what led to their deaths. Silly people...silly, silly people. It was just a matter of time.

Chapter 25

Mike gave the information to his safe source to check the facial recognition, avoided his office, and headed back to the safe house. He stopped along the way at a grocery store he would not usually have gone to, making sure to keep his own head covered with a hat. He bought Maggie some of the Jarlsberg cheese he remembered she had loved on the island. He bought Reggie her favorite kind of candy bars, and Connie her coffee. He also got a bottle of wine, but it was just for "The Ladies." No drinking for him tonight, as he was on the job.

Mike took a different route to the safe house and pulled his car into the garage of the spare condo. He had looked down the street to see if he could see anyone, but the street was quiet, except for the same cars that had been there often before. All the plates had checked out, and it was just locals living in the community.

Mike walked in the door with his wonderful bag of hot fried chicken and biscuits. He knew this horrible situation had a non-horrible moment when he thought about sitting down with Maggie and having dinner. His stomach growled, which got a laugh from all as he helped set the table.

Their dinner was fun and interesting as Mike recounted the day with Bobbi and saw the hopeful look on Maggie's face. "Maybe we can get this guy sooner than we thought," he said. "I'll show you her tape, but I'm worried that if I found her, our bomber may find her as well. I placed a car down the street from her, but I'm still not sure if that was smart, because if our leak is in our department and this guy checks out all of our cars, we're doomed." He laughed and said, "Now we'll probably get some neighbor calling in saying there's a pervert on their street."

They all laughed, finished their dinner, and cleaned up. Connie joined them for a few minutes to eat, because she took her job very seriously. Connie's replacements came for duty. Both Connie and her replacement were fine tuned to hear a pin drop outside the condo. The cameras did not show the entire condo. Connie was in a separate room with the door closed monitoring the front door, front hallway, and down the street. She even had her own little refrigerator inside the room.

***

Mike showed them the surveillance clip, and again Reggie felt a nagging feeling that she had seen the bomber somewhere before.

"Okay, you guys. I'm headed to my room to write some more and just chill. See you tomorrow."

CHAPTER 26

"See you, Reggie," Mike and Maggie said together.

Feeling relaxed but not intoxicated after one glass of wine, Maggie sat on the couch with Mike. They started to chat about their lives, Maggie's children, their work, and all the things that a couple might talk about in their living room.

Every once in a while Maggie would see a glint in Mike's eye as he told a story, and smiled. During one story, it was as if they both realized they were having a wonderful time just sitting together. When the clock chimed ten o'clock, both of them were surprised at how long they had been sitting there.

"Guess I better head next door," Mike said, getting up from the couch.

"Yes, I'd better hit the hay soon, too. It's been a long day," Maggie said, feeling happy.

Maggie was walking behind Mike when he suddenly turned and muttered, "Screw the rules," and drew her into his arms, kissing her hard on the lips. She tilted her chin up and kissed him passionately, wrapping her arms around his waist.

Both of them moved towards the bedroom as they continued to feel their bodies getting hot with desire. As they stumbled onto the bed, Mike began removing Maggie's clothes slowly and tenderly as he kissed her neck and moved his lips slowly up to hers. He felt hungry for her body, and their kisses grew more intense as she began to quickly undress Mike. He pulled Maggie's beautiful naked body against him as he entered her, and they began to move in a slow and steady rhythm. The rhythm grew faster and faster until the force of their lovemaking and explosion of their desire left them exhausted and breathless.

As they lay in each other's arms, Mike kissed her and whispered, "I could get used to this, Maggie Andrews."

Maggie tilted her head up to look into his eyes, and whispered, "Me, too."

They held each other close and drifted off.

CHAPTER 27

Somewhere else in town, the bad guy banged his fist on the table. I will find them, and soon. It will be HER fault that someone close to her has to die. All he wanted to do was do his job, get his money, and not have some woman get the best of him. Women had always gotten the best of him in life. His grandmother, who was supposed to be watching him while his father worked, spent her life drunk and surely thinking of ways to humiliate him. As soon as his father would walk out the door, her smile would turn to a sneer and she would stick him in front of the television and pass out on the couch. She would make him a sandwich before she got drunk and put it on the coffee table with a glass of soda. She always set the alarm to awaken before his father came home. Day after day she would tell his father what a mean boy he was, and that he was lucky she watched him, because no one else would want to watch such a bad boy. "Mark my words, he will end up in jail unless you do something." And what made him even more furious was that his dad believed her. Most kids played baseball with their dads, but his dad's idea of quality time was spending hours in the basement teaching him all about bombs, like his dad had learned in the service. The only time his father seemed proud of him was when he finally became a bomb expert. The world did not know, but his dad knew his skill. Now, his grandmother and dad were both dead, but he could still hear their voices in his head.

Once he went to school he had a teacher or two who would tell him what a nice boy he was, but by then it was too late. The bad voices in him were getting louder and louder. People would never know that he was a bad man. Yes, people would be surprised that he had a wife, but even she had no idea of his past, or his bomb making. He was just a nice guy to her, not the bomber he truly was.

He started to think of his grandmother and dad again, and other things that could have made him want to smash a wall, but he forced himself to focus and think how he was going to find where she was hidden.

And he would find out. Oh, yes. He would find out.

Chapter 28

Mike woke up in his condo next to the safe house with the insistence of his alarm yelling at him to get up. He could still smell the scent of Maggie's body, and it made him want to have her next to him, not just to make love, but to feel her warmth.

He'd hated that he had to leave her bed to come back to his. It felt so right with her. Suddenly he felt a little embarrassed. What if she came to her senses today and did not want to see him again? He could understand that, and yet he could already feel the ache in his heart if that was to happen.

He got out of bed, quickly showered, and headed over to the safe house. Connie had already changed shifts, so it was Steven who was watching him as he approached the door. Connie may have told him of Mike's behavior the night before, but he didn't care this time. It was Maggie's face he couldn't wait to see, and her reaction.

The two ladies were at the table sipping their coffee when

Mike walked in. Maggie smiled at him with a big smile, yet there was a question in the smile for him.

"Morning, you two. I don't have time for breakfast, but thought I would stop in and say bye before I headed out to the station," Mike said, giving a special nod to Maggie and moving closer to her. "You two be safe today, and don't worry. I think we have a good chance of getting our guy. And if we can place a person in the company, our chances get better."

"Bye, Mike," both women said, with Maggie getting up to walk him to the door.

"Really, be safe. We can take care of ourselves, so don't worry," Maggie said, touching his hand and giving it a light squeeze.

"I will," he said, gently squeezing her hand, not wanting to let go.

Mike headed out the door after checking in with Sam. He walked down the street to his car that he had parked in a hidden spot, and slid into the driver's seat. Before he could turn the key in the ignition, a voice from the back seat said "Stop."

Mike started to whip his head around when he felt an arm go around his neck.

"Just relax," said the voice behind him.

"Shit," Mike said as he felt the hand tighten around his neck. *Relax, my ass, I'm about to get killed.* His next thought was of Maggie, and how ironic that he had finally found another someone and it was too late.

"I'm not going to hurt you," the voice said, pulling his arm away from Mike. "My name is Agent Sine," he said pulling out his badge and showing it to Mike, who was still feeling sweaty and still felt his heart racing. "I just want you to know that your prying may blow the biggest case we have had on animal trafficking in this country. I've planted myself for the last six months in the company, and we are so close to getting the CEO. We know the guy you're looking for had a hand in something that went on in Minnesota, but we don't know who this guy is yet. I'm a special agent working with various agencies to nab this ring. There has always been animal smuggling into this country, but our lady who owns the company here is the queen of queens of this. There have been deaths around the country, and we would like to see if there is any connection, but I'd hit a dead end till our bombing here. She must have put her trained assassin's personal information somewhere. She's meticulous and careful, but she must have something somewhere…she is too smart not to."

Mike looked at the man in the back seat carefully, surprised by his yuppie appearance; tan slacks, striped shirt, tie, and trimmed blond hair. Just your average business guy.

"We'll keep you in the loop, but I can't risk you guys trying to bring your own person into the company."

"How will I get to you?" Mike asked.

"You don't. I'll get to you," the man said, his face an expressionless mask. "We are literally about to bust this wide open any day now, and you can't mess it up."

"What about the FBI?"

"They know all about this, at least the top brass. We're trying not to have too many people involved. Mrs. Andrews opened a can of worms when she was there for the bombing. That's enough said for today. Sorry I scared you," the man said, with a look that said "I'm really not sorry at all." As he started to step out of the car, he turned to Mike and said, "I found you because we heard you might bring in someone. Just think what would have happened if it had been 'our guy' in the back seat instead of me."

Mike felt a sense of dread, and an even stronger determination to find out who the killer was. Maybe he did need to get Maggie and Reggie out of town. He'd thought they would be totally safe, but this was a different ballgame. There was always the other safe place no one in the force knew about…his cabin in the woods that not even his buddies knew about. It was left to him by a distant relative, and no records were on file linking him to it. He used to go there every weekend with his wife, but had not been there in years. It was more than a cabin to Mike, but a home filled with wonderful memories. A neighbor up there kept an eye on it, and his neighbor's son had rented it from him this past year for whatever he could afford for the month. He had just moved to Atlanta, so his neighbor had cleaned the place, painted it, and it was the perfect place to hide Maggie and Reggie.

CHAPTER 29

Mike watched the agent disappear into his car and pull away.

He jumped out of his car and ran up to the condo, ringing the bell as he yelled into the speaker. "Let me in, Steven."

Steven came to the door running and opened it. Mike muttered thanks as he hurried down the hall.

Maggie and Reggie stood up quickly from the table, and after seeing the look of panic and determination on Mike's face, they stood very still.

"Time to go, ladies…NOW."

"What?" they both said, looking confused.

"You need to pack your bags, NOW. I think we may have been compromised, and I need to get you somewhere safer."

"Has someone found us…the bomber?" Reggie said, not able to hide the panic in her voice.

"Yes, he may have. I'll explain everything in the car. No one knows we are heading out or where. Now, please pack."

Mike said in a voice that had Maggie and Reggie turning to run to their bedrooms.

Someone could be outside and waiting for them to leave. If the agent could find him, it might be too late. If the leak was someone he knew, they could all be dead.

Maggie and Reggie finished packing and headed out the door and to the car with Mike. They drove for a few minutes in silence before Mike filled them in on all that had happened that morning. Maggie was sitting next to him, so at one point he touched her shoulder lightly as he spoke, and he felt better just to feel her next to him.

It took about twenty minutes to get up to his cabin through winding roads, and as they turned down a narrow dirt road, they saw a deer standing by the side of the road with her two fawns. When they heard the car coming closer, their white tails went up and she gave them her high pitched mother sound as they bounded away from the car. The gravel crunched under the tires, and since it had been a hot summer all the ferns along the way were brownish from the draught. The fire alert was high this time, and Mike always hoped his cabin would not go up in flames if someone lit a cigarette and threw it out of the car. *I would be crushed*, he thought, his chest tightening as he put those thoughts out of his mind.

As they drove further and further back, they started to see cottages along the way. There was his friend Pete's cabin, next door to Mrs. Simmons's, and the young couple's place a little down the river.

His place was actually a real beauty. It was a white cabin with black trim that all the neighbors admired. The inside was cozy and restful, and it was near a cliff overlooking the river, which made Mike want to retire here someday and fish. But it was the smell of the fresh pine trees that he missed in the city the most.

"This is gorgeous, Mike," Maggie said, still in shock from the sudden move, but taken aback by the beauty of the forest and the cabin.

"This is gorgeous, all right," Reggie said, "but here we are, in the middle of nowhere, and how am I supposed to stay in communication with my station?"

"That's why I told you to tell your crew and relatives that you were going on vacation for a while and could only be reached through my office for emergencies. We are very close to getting our guy, and he is very close to getting us, I'm afraid."

They all headed up the stairs onto the porch and into the cabin. Mike assigned each of them a room, and he was going to use the small screened in porch to be his room and lookout.

Night would be settling in. He looked around the grounds to see if anything had been tampered with, knowing that the only way a person could find them here was if they traced their cells. He hadn't told anyone about this place, and he wasn't going to. He would ask Mrs. Stanley to keep an eye on his friends when he went to work. Although she was seventy-five, she was not one to be messed with and did not have loose lips.

***

Maggie was getting mad now. She was scared, of course, but this jerk was playing with her. There was no way she was going to end up dead, or let him hurt anyone else. She had been Mrs. Nice Guy and felt like a victim, but she could feel the fury running in her veins now.

"Mike, do you have any guns here?" Maggie asked.

"Yes. Why do you ask?"

"If he should find us, I swear I'm going to blow him away."

"Oh, come on, Maggie. You're not really thinking of killing him?" Reggie asked, looking at Mike to say something that would make Maggie come to her senses.

"I will try if he really is planning to kill us," Maggie said to them both. "I know, me, Miss Social Worker, talking about blowing someone away, but this man is a killer, a trained killer. I hope the police catch him and lock him away forever, and of course I'm frightened, but this has gone on too long."

***

Mike didn't say much as he headed back to his car. There was part of him that agreed with Maggie, but if the killer ever got that close to her, it may not be *him* that was blown away. This was the perfect place to teach Reggie how to shoot.

Mike headed back to town, and Reggie and Maggie used the throw away phone to let their families know they were okay. They pored through the files in the afternoon, and both came to the conclusion that the financial company the dead man worked for was their connection. Someone there must know something. It started to get dark, and both Reggie and Maggie shuddered at the same time, both thinking that they were out in the middle of nowhere, and both feeling a sense of unease being without Mike. Yet, both knew if push came to shove they would survive.

Mike came back later that evening. They all headed to bed, Mike and Maggie resisting the urge to be with each other. The hug they gave each other in front of Reggie told her how much they had begun to care about one another. They all had the feeling that the peacefulness was not something that would last forever.

CHAPTER 30

The CEO sat in the back of her limo, sipping her favorite cocktail as she headed home from work. The whole situation had gotten rather messy.

She had trusted her employee to fix everything like he always had through the years, but he had gotten too cocky and had made a mistake. She loved that he was bad, but she also hated the fact, too. She had never thought he would screw up. He'd never screwed up…until now. He had kept the hounds off her door for years, and had been very loyal. Yes, she loved that he was loyal, and could be called upon to fly across the country and nicely "fix" any problems that came along. Years ago she had met him at a conference before he was married, and there was something in his eyes that scared and delighted her. They had had a brief fling, for the sake of sex only, and after seeing his true side, she approached him carefully to be her "fixer." He had acted shocked, but then she saw his eyes light up with humor and he smiled broadly as he realized she was serious. Now, besides making money, he could be his *real* self.

After they kissed to seal their deal and made the arrangements as to how this situation would be, he started his "other job." Never again did they have sex, kiss, or greet each other in any manner other than politely if they ran into each other. She married, and divorced. He met his wife, got married, avoided kids, and complained to his "friends" how boring life could be at times. No one knew about him except for the CEO. She was the only one who could contact him in their usual secretive manner. She did have one other who helped with the smuggling, but he was dead now, due to his stupidity. What a moron to take the computer to be fixed. But the killer had solved that, set a bomb, and then got rid of him. She even had him search the dead man's house to make sure nothing was there that could lead the police to them. Her fixer had been helping her with her animal business through the years, and had helped her be a very wealthy woman. She had never told anyone about him, had nothing written down, and knew they would take this secret to their graves if he didn't screw up. She was a pillar of the community, she laughed to herself, trying to get in a joyful mood again. She wondered how people would feel if they knew she was a criminal. *He'd better not screw up again*, she pouted as she took a sip of her drink.

The slight sound of shattering glass was the last thing the CEO heard before she slumped onto the seat.

***

The killer felt a sense of relief. Another woman who had been causing him problems was gone. He should feel a little bad about killing her after all these years...but he didn't.

Now there was no one to trace him to any of these crimes. There was only one woman he needed to get rid of now, then he would be free.

It was so silly that they didn't think he could find them. He would get her, he promised himself, within the next forty-eight hours. This was his last thing to fix, and he had enough money to live in this crappy city and still travel around the world with his wife. She was the only one he trusted, and she fortunately was not smart enough to realize his "other side."

He got his things ready to go to the police station the next day… so easy…no one would suspect him…so easy.

CHAPTER 31

The police station buzzed with activity as the man with the uniform and baseball cap with the long brim almost covering his eyes casually walked in and over to the desk.

"Hey Joe, is Sam in today? I have a package for him."

"He's here, but he's real busy, Tim. Let me take it for him," Joe said, having received many packages from Tim through the years. Whenever they wanted something delivered, all they had to do was call Tim's service and he rushed over. Tim's business probably went through rough times with the economy, but Tim was always so friendly that the guys at the station trusted him.

"That will be great, and I have something for Mike. Is he in today?"

"He's out in the field, but he should be in shortly to pick up his mail. You want to wait, Tim?"

"No, I've got to go. Is he on vacation?" Tim asked casually.

"No, he is working on a tough case, and keeping a low

profile."

"He's a lucky guy...he gets to work from his home."

"He's somewhere else, but I have no idea where...one of those top secret things," Joe winked. "Have you and your wife been on any more trips? You're lucky you're able to travel a little. I'm stuck behind this desk. But hey, man, at least I have a job."

Tim smiled. "Just give him this, please. Later."

Tim laughed, dropped off the packages, and headed outside as casually as he'd come in. He had made a dummy package and filled it with candy, with a typed note thanking Mike for being such a good detective. When he got into his truck with the not so clear window, he carefully peeled off his fingerprints. He would wait for Mike and follow him, and try to see where he was going.

He was so close to ending this. Thank God his wife was out of town...he was tempted to go visit the woman he had seen before, but he had broken it off, and she certainly wasn't a fan of his. He did not need any distractions now, even though it would be great sex.

CHAPTER 32

Mike got up and left Maggie and Reggie again. He pulled into the back lot at the police station and walked into the building through the side door. He had to fill in the team about what was going on, but he was surprised by the buzz of agents in the conference room as he entered.

"What's going on?" Mike asked.

"The head of that company was found with one shot to her head in the back of her limo. Her driver was killed also. Our guy must have thought she may turn on him. I will say this guy is one smart, calculating son of a bitch. We are getting all the web cams and traffic cams, but my bet is this guy picked a spot where we couldn't get him coming or going on camera. This town is ideal for him, not too big and yet not too small… perfect for a murderer."

"You had her under surveillance. What happened?"

"We had her office bugged, had someone watching outside her house, but we had no idea this would happen on her way home. We're checking all her phone records like we have been, but this lady was no fool. She probably had burner phones. Our guys are trying to look at all the info and see if one number keeps popping up, but so far it's a dead end. Now that she's dead, we're going over her computer with a fine toothed comb, and her house is being searched from top to bottom. Took the judge only one hour to approve the warrant with all the evidence we gave him."

Mike thought about what Maggie had said about the guy, and that he might be an average person who worked with the CEO. "Have we looked into all the employees?"

"Long time ago, Mike," an agent said. "No one seems to be our guy. I'm embarrassed to say we didn't know that the man who was killed had something to do with the smuggling. We were getting so close, and now that we found the hidden envelope in our dead guy's place we were going to move in and arrest the CEO, and do a country wide sting. The sting is happening as we speak. We knew if we didn't take quick action, the others would be 'in the wind.' But our guy's a ghost. No mention of him anywhere."

"What about people who didn't work for the company, but had regular dealings with them? If our guy is local, he wouldn't get a lot of attention."

"We've looked into that some, but nothing's come up so far. Now that the CEO is dead, we are going into the company and interviewing the people to see what we can get, or maybe one of them is our guy."

Mike looked at his watch and realized that he needed to head out of town quickly. After reading his mail and smiling at a box of candy someone had sent, he left through the back door. He looked both ways but didn't see anything suspicious, so he got into his car and headed out. He stopped briefly to pick up some groceries and headed up to the cabin.

***

Mike was unaware of the van keeping its distance from him as it followed him. When Mike turned off onto a small gravel road, the van kept going.

"Gotcha." the killer said to himself with a broad smile. "Now you just have to leave and she's all mine." He couldn't believe the detective hadn't checked for a tracking device on his car before he left. The killer had waited in the parking lot, knowing what Mike looked like, but Mike had no idea who he was when he parked in a side lot and went in the back door. What did this detective think he was, stupid? Who's the stupid one this time? He laughed. "Got you," he started saying in a sing song voice and laughing...like he did when he was a kid...and like he did before he did something bad.

TOO LATE TO RUN

CHAPTER 33

Maggie and Reggie had spent some of the day looking at files, but it felt like they were at a dead end. To clear their brains they went out to the back of the cabin that had a slope down to the river. On one side of the cabin there were two vacant lots with a clearing. On the other side was Mrs. Stanley's house. Maggie figured the clearing would be a good place to teach Reggie how to shoot. They were far enough from other houses that the bullets would not ricochet and go through any windows or hurt people. Mike must have used this spot for his own target practice, as there was a board with a figure of a head tacked to it. Maggie went up to the board and saw that if that had been someone's brain, Mike would have taken them out quickly. She began by giving Reggie lots of safety tips, and spent much time going over how guns work. She had always been slightly afraid of guns, and was very concerned about someone getting accidently hurt. Now for the first time she felt some power over her fears of the killer.

Reggie was a quick learner, and after one hour and sore fingers, she felt she could use a gun if she had to. Both Reggie and Maggie had had martial arts training, but Maggie had had it years before and did not feel like she remembered much. Reggie remembered most of the moves, but both of the women wished they would never be in the position where they had to use them.

They heard a car coming up the drive and, per Mike's instructions, they hid until they could see who it was driving up. Out came Mike, groceries in hand, looking even more serious than when he had left that morning. "Oh, my God," Maggie said to Reggie, "Something must have happened." Maggie went over to Mike quickly. "Hi, Mike. All okay?"

"Not really," he frowned. "That CEO we were going to investigate was shot, and we're almost sure it was by our killer."

"How was she shot?" Reggie asked, shocked.

"A bullet to the head from a distance as she was riding home in her limo," Mike said. "If it is him, and he killed his boss, he's getting out of control and has nothing to lose. This makes me more afraid for you both. We're getting closer to finding this guy, and someone or a camera is going to give us a clue. We have just put up a reward of $10,000 for the CEO's killer that will help us get our guy. In the meantime, around the country and abroad, they are rounding up what operations may have been involved with this smuggling before they scatter."

"Mike, this is too big of news for me to keep quiet on." Reggie insisted. "I need to call in any information only our station is privileged to. Can I say there is a reward, or that there may be some connection between our guy and the killing of the CEO?"

162

"You can break the story of the reward, Reggie. In fact, I told the team that this was yours first. But you can't show up there in person at the station, not now. Don't get your hopes up of us finding him. Our guy has just been profiled by the best the FBI has. He says he is an average guy you would not suspect. He would be pleasant, charming, probably handsome, liked by his neighbors, maybe married, travels out of town yet knows this town like the back of his hand, and someone no one would suspect. Yet they think that someone has seen this other side of him, or a slight glimpse, and this is the person who is going to give him to us. Plus, someone must have noticed this guy had bomb making material or guns somewhere, we hope."

"How big is the team taking calls, Mike?" Reggie asked.

"We have about three people available for calls, even on the night shift. I'm going back there tonight to work the phones. I will send Sam up here to be with you both. He is the only one I trust to know where you are. It feels like the killer is getting desperate, and this is too far out and desolate for you guys to be here alone. I know my neighbor knows you're here, and she is a tough old dame, but let's not take any chances."

Reggie quickly used her phone to call the station and worked on a scoop about the reward that would quickly get on the news. In fact, they were going to break into the regular programming and announce information about the killing. Reggie had to keep walking from place to place outside as the reception for her phone kept dropping.

Mike, Maggie, and Reggie unloaded the groceries and talked of their gun shooting practice during lunch, and then Mike headed back to town. Maggie walked him to his car and he gave her a gentle kiss. "You stay safe, Maggie Andrews," he said with a mixture of caring and fear.

"I will, Mike," she said quietly as she squeezed his hand and brought it to her heart. "Stay safe."

She watched him get into his car and heard the gravel hit his tires as the car winded down the road. She kept waving in case he was watching, and she felt sick to her stomach inside. *Oh, please let us all be safe. Please let someone find this monster so this nightmare ends.*

Her mind shifted to her sons, and she was happy they were away from all this. She felt even more determined to keep her and Reggie safe up here. The thought of something happening to her, and her sons having to deal with it, was something she was not willing to live with. She would help to get this killer.

Maggie walked back inside to begin the slow process of looking through files with Reggie until Sam came up. Maybe there was one that she would open and see an eye, a chin, and a look, and know it was the killer.

The neighbor, Mrs. Stanley, knocked on the door that afternoon and had a plate of cookies in her hand. She came in to chat with Reggie and Maggie for a short while, but said she could only stay a few minutes, and then went back to her place. She had known Mike for years, and she said she would keep her ears open for anything strange happening or any strangers coming by. She said of course she had seen the news and recognized Maggie and Reggie, but she wasn't about to tell anyone else. She had lived up here for a long time, and she wasn't scared easily. Maggie and Reggie looked at the frail but determined woman and hoped she wasn't sucked into this mess.

Just as Mrs. Stanley was about to leave, a car came down the road and into their U shaped driveway in front of the cabin. For an instant all three froze in place, but then the women recognized Sam.

***

"It's Sam," Reggie said, relieved to see him. He came to the door and Reggie let him in and introduced him to Mrs. Stanley. Sam had never been to Mike's place, but he did not like the fact it was isolated, surrounded by woods and the stone cliff overlooking the river.

Great for getting away and to see nature, but not so great if someone is trying to kill you, Sam thought.

Mrs. Stanley left for her home. Maggie and Reggie began to look at the contents of the big box that Sam had brought. They had expected files, but Sam had brought yearbooks from the local high school.

"Yearbooks?" Reggie said, confused, looking at Sam as he joined them at the table.

"I figure our guy must know someone here, and I also started to wonder, maybe he is a local. I don't have all the yearbooks, but got the ones from the library with people who might be around our killer's age. I know he uses disguises, and you really didn't get a good look at his face, but maybe we'll get lucky. Good thing our town has only one high school, and has a library that hasn't scanned all these into their computer. They kept them in the basement, and these go back years." Sam shrugged. "It's worth a try."

Maggie and Reggie agreed and started to go through the yearbooks. Sam excused himself to look around the cabin. He was getting uneasy, and was not comfortable that there seemed to be only one entrance. He wanted to know if there was another way out, or for that matter, another way into the cabin. He was about resigned that the front door, sliding glass door, and windows were it, when he spotted another door. "Hey, where does this door go?" he asked, while turning the

165

handle.

"We haven't been down there, but Mike said it leads to the root cellar. Mike used to store food down there. He said there is an entrance to the root cellar from outside, but it's padlocked and he doesn't use it."

"I'm going to check it out. It's always good to have another way to get out if you need it," Sam said cheerfully. Sam did not want to scare the women, but he did know with this vicious killer their life depended on having a Plan B to get away if he found them.

"I'd like to see it, too," Reggie said, getting up, which prompted Maggie to say, "Me, too."

They walked down the very old stone steps and came out in a small room with many shelves and a very low ceiling, causing Sam to bend over as he walked across the room to avoid a hard hit to his head. The cellar was cold and damp and would have been the perfect place to store things from a garden, but now it was filled with garden tools, old framed pictures, and big empty barrels. The few steps up at the other end led to two wooden doors that opened to the yard. Sam walked up the steps and fiddled with the lock. *Damn*, he thought, *locked*. Mike must have put the key somewhere down here. Sam ran his hand along the wall by the steps, and in one tiny corner, he felt it rub against a nail and felt a key.

"If you ever need to use this door, the key is here. I'm going to leave it here, but come over and feel where it is." Sam could see the blossoming fear creep onto their faces, even in the low light of the basement. "Don't worry. He's not going to come down here, but it's always good to know every possible exit, just in case."

They felt the key's location also. Sam was about to try it out when they heard some faint sound outside. He calmly said it was time to go upstairs and finish the yearbooks, all the while planning how to check out the noise if he heard it again. He wanted the ladies to be prepared, but not panic. *A raccoon is probably out there,* he thought, looking for food, or what sounded like a raccoon.

Sam did take a quick look outside when they went back up, but everything looked in order.

It was still light out, but it would be dark in a few hours. Time went by, and besides a break for dinner they continued looking at the yearbooks. Every once in a while Sam would automatically brush his hand over his gun. He was in uniform and took his assignment very seriously.

***

They were all disappointed that they had not found anything, when Maggie said, "Oh, my God, no. This couldn't be him."

She was looking at one of the yearbook's candid pictures, and there was something about the picture that showed three guys standing outside the school's field that made her heart race. No name, nothing but a side profile, yet it was such a familiar side profile. Maggie looked back at all the individual profiles and group pictures, but she could not be sure. It was just that side profile that she could almost be sure of…almost. Maybe she just wanted to find something, she told herself, and it was probably not the bomber.

"Great, Maggie," Sam said, as he and Reggie came over to stare at the picture too. "If I can find someone who went to high school that year, we might be able to nail this guy's identity…*If* it is our guy. I'll tell Mike the year we're looking at and he can take it from there." Sam texted Mike, and then all three took a break just to sit down on the couch and relax, telling each other funny stories to ease the tension. With no

167

lights outside to lighten the sky when looking outside, all they saw was the sky becoming darker and darker.

***

At the same time, Mrs. Stanley was cleaning up from her dinner of scrambled eggs and cheese. Since she lived alone she did not have to worry about cooking big dinners, but could make herself something quick, and like tonight, eat as late as she wanted. Often she added a glass of wine and sat down to watch television and relax for the evening. She kept the television volume low because she wanted to make sure she could hear her neighbors if they needed her. She had promised Mike she would look out for them, so she would. He was like a son to her, since she had no husband, children, or sisters and brothers. Her parents were long gone, and her husband had died over twenty years ago, so it was just her.

As she settled back into her chair, she heard the faintest sound that she had never heard before. When she had first moved into her place all the noises would scare her, but now she knew every sound, and they were almost comforting to her. Yet, this sound was a new one. She traced the sound to outside and figured it was a new critter out there. She got her broom out to scare the thing away and headed to the door. She looked out the window, but saw nothing. Mrs. Stanley had this sudden uncomfortable feeling that something was wrong…very wrong. She quickly called the number Mike had left her for Maggie, but she was unable to get through. *Must be something about the service and connection*, she thought. She was using her landline, so she called Mike to ask him if he could get through to Maggie. She just had this bad feeling and wanted to see if all was okay. Mike's voice mail came on, and she left a quick message. "Drat," she said, getting irritated and afraid. "Why can't I get through to anyone?"

168

She knew she could not just wonder anymore, and threw on her sweater to head over to Mike's cabin. As she stepped onto her porch, banging the door to scare any animals away, she saw someone coming towards her. *Thank goodness they are coming so I can ask them how they are*, she thought with relief.

As she started to greet her visitor, she heard the faintest pop before she fell to the porch in a pile. Her last thoughts as she looked down at her wound was, *Oh, no, he found Maggie…* along with a deep sadness…she had let Mike down.

Chapter 34

Mike was getting lots of calls about the killer since they'd posted a reward, when he decided to take fifteen minutes away from the phone and eat his dinner. He rarely turned his phone off, but he felt he needed fifteen minutes of peace. One of their leads said they knew who the guy was, and if they got the reward, they would tell them. They did not want to meet, but wanted the reward. It was a woman, and by her voice Mike could tell that she knew the man she was talking about, and sure was angry at him. Maybe it was another person trying to get even with someone having nothing to do with the killing, or maybe someone who really did know the guy. She hung up fast before they could trace the call, and said she would call tomorrow morning. He would also pursue the lead Sam had said about a local.

Mike finished his usual quick dinner from the only food truck they had in the city, which happened to be parked out front tonight, and headed back to his desk. On the way in he turned his phone back on and saw there was a message from Mrs. Stanley. He quickly hit a button and listened to her message. "Mike, this is Mrs. Stanley. I wonder if you could contact Maggie. I'm sure she's fine, but I heard a strange noise and I can't get through to her by phone. I'm going over there now to see if she's okay."

Mike immediately called Sam's phone and got an answer. "Hey Sam, I got a call from Mrs. Stanley. She said she heard something, but couldn't get through to Maggie. Does her phone have reception?"

"No, Maggie can't use her phone. Reggie either, but mine seems to be fine," Sam told him. "Their phones are going in and out. All seems to be okay here, Mike."

"What about Mrs. Stanley?" Mike asked. "She was going to come over and see if all was okay. Can I speak to her?"

Sam said, "Sorry, Mike. She's not here. Are you sure she said she was coming over? What was the noise she heard?"

"I don't know," Mike said, feeling more and more uneasy. "Mrs. Stanley wouldn't say she was going to come over and not show. She may have tripped, or gotten hurt. Could you just go over to her house and make sure she's okay?"

"Sure I will. I'll check in with you right after I speak with her."

***

Maggie and Reggie looked expectantly at him when he got off the phone, and asked what was going on.

"There's something wrong with Mrs. Stanley. She left Mike a message that she was coming over here. I'm going over to check her house. Lock the door after me. I'll be right back." He gave Reggie a special smile that made her grin back. *Damn, he is a fine man,* she thought, as she made sure she knew where her gun was.

171

***

Sam started to walk down the side path that led to Mrs. Stanley's house. He was glad it was a straight path, unlike the twisted one that led down to the river with the ledge overlooking it. As he got closer to the house, he became aware that there were no sounds, just total darkness, and only the light of his flashlight leading the way. *Too dark*, Sam thought, *but I'm almost there.*

Finally, he saw the porch light, the only light on in the house. As he got closer he saw what looked like some sort of animal feed bag on the porch. Sam shone his flashlight onto the bag.

"Shit," he said, as he jumped back for a minute. He realized it was Mrs. Stanley, a pool of blood spreading from her leg. He put his fingers to her neck, hoping to feel a pulse, but she was dead.

Sam grabbed his phone, turned off his flashlight, and raced off the porch in a zigzag safety run toward Mike's cabin. He quickly dialed Mike's number.

"Mike, we need help. Mrs. Stanley is dead." He heard a bullet fly past his head and drew his gun, but in the dark had no idea where the killer was situated. But he knew he was there. And he wanted them all dead.

He darted up to the cabin door and pounded on it. "Maggie, Reggie, he's here, the bomber is here," he screamed. Reggie and Maggie ran to let him in when they heard a shot and saw his back arch. Blood oozed down his shirt as he stumbled down the porch onto the grass, trying to divert the bombers attention to him.

Sam opened his eyes and looked at Reggie, mouthing, *"RUN."*

***

For some odd reason, the bomber felt very calm. He was finally in control again. He knew his targets would panic and run out the cabin's side door, in full view. He would have even more fun setting fire to the cabin and seeing how long it would take them to come out. He had a surprise for Maggie, though. She had made his life so miserable that he did not want her to die too quickly...she must suffer, and he would figure out how later. But now, he kept his eye on the door and waited, tempted to taunt them to come out, but deciding to keep silent for now. He lit the firebomb fuse, threw it at the cabin, and watched the timber start to burn.

CHAPTER 35

"Go, go," Maggie said, shoving Reggie forward and grabbing the gun and tucking it into her waistband. They both hid behind the couch, waiting for the killer to come in after them. As they waited, they could smell wood burning. "Oh, no, he's set the cabin on fire. We have to get out of here."

They were about to head out the door when Maggie said, "Stop, he wants us to run out to him. Let's go to the root cellar. He doesn't know about the key."

Maggie and Reggie ran into the dark cellar and did not turn on the light. Reggie used the dim light of her cell phone to help them along. Maggie's hand was shaking as she tried to find the key. *Nothing*, she thought. Where was that key? They could begin to smell the smoke coming into the basement and they felt their eyes sting. Reggie kept trying to call out on her cell phone to get help, but the line was dead. "Let me find that damn key," Maggie said to Reggie. One more time she ran her hands over the wall, and finally her hand closed around the nail with the key. She grabbed it and took Reggie's hand and led her up the stairs to the door.

"We have to open this quietly," Maggie whispered. "Thank God Mike put the padlock on the inside."

Smoke was thickening the cellar air as Maggie put the key in the lock. Unable to control her coughing, Maggie struggled to turn the key and, as the intense heat from the fire penetrated into the cellar, the lock opened. Her hands sweating from fear, she quickly slipped it off and said to Reggie, "Push it open and *RUN*...just run...don't stop to shoot, just run...."

The door sprung open and they ran away from the cabin. The path to the river by the cliff was the closest, and they sprinted in that direction.

***

As the fire burned the cabin, the killer waited by the door. Suddenly, in the fire's glow he saw the women running. "What the hell?" he could not stop from yelling, his state of happiness at the thought of killing them disappearing. The happiness changed to rage as he chased them down the path.

***

"I know that below the clearing where we practiced today is the river. We could hide in the woods, but if we get to the river and a boat, we might escape," Maggie said.

They scrambled towards the river. As they got to the clearing, they hesitated while trying to find the path to the river, and a shot rang out. Reggie made a guttural sound and fell to the ground. Maggie saw Reggie's leg was hit and quickly pulled her into the ferns by the trees. "I'll be back, Reggie, don't make a sound," she whispered.

Reggie squeezed her hand and then let go. *Please get back, Reggie* thought. *I'm not ready to die. Get the son of a bitch.*

***

175

Maggie was going to stay with Reggie, but decided the best thing for Reggie was for Maggie to maneuver the bomber away from her, and draw him towards her. She hoped to get to the boat she had seen from afar when they had target practice, but her legs were weak from running and fear.

She stumbled into the clearing and ran towards the boat. She felt a sharp pain on her left forearm and looked down to see blood pouring out.

"Oh no you don't, you bastard," she yelled. "I'm not going to let you kill me like you did my friends."

She got into the boat and picked up the oar. She saw a light of a house nearby and was going to try to get to it in the total darkness that surrounded her. Suddenly she felt a hand grab her bleeding arm and pull her out of the boat with such force she thought she was being thrown into the air. The pain was so intense she tried to fight back, but couldn't.

"Oh, don't worry, Maggie," the stranger said. "I'm not going to kill you yet. I want you to suffer like I have suffered. I want to make this last. I just want you to stay alive a while," he laughed. "Your friends are dead, and even if one is still alive, I'll kill them later."

When he mentioned he would kill them, she felt an intense hate and strength well up in her. When they got to the top of the cliff, he let her hand go and kicked her in her side. He then kicked her a few more times, and then once in the head.

CHAPTER 36

As she started to slip into unconsciousness, there seemed to be fog and Maggie could only hear a voice that sounded much like her late husband Henry's voice saying softly, "You'll be okay, Maggie. You're strong. You must wake up."

"Oh, my God, is it you, Henry?" Maggie said softly as tears started running down her cheeks. A face appeared very close to hers, and it was Henry holding her close.

"I have missed you so much, Henry. Is this a dream?"

His curly brown hair and green eyes locked on hers, and she felt a sense of peace she had not known since he died. All those years together, two children together, and being each other's best friend played before her like a movie on a screen. First kiss, wedding, first fight, kids, seeing Mount Rushmore, graduations, and most of all laughing together, and her feeling her heart race when he walked in the door.

"I miss you, but I'm always with you. You can't stay…. You must go back, you must be happy, you must fight."

Henry had tears in his eyes. *This must be a dream*, Maggie thought, because no one ever said angels in heaven cry.

Henry slowly let go of Maggie and she felt his kiss softly on her lips. "No, Henry, not yet," and she fell into darkness.

Maggie woke up in pain with tears on her cheeks, and when she opened her eyes she saw the killer smiling and sitting on a big rock near her.

"I didn't think you were going to wake up. No one will miss you…what a pain you are. No one will know I'm the killer. Your stupid detective will search and search, and he won't find any clues. Your body will wash down the river, and if I'm lucky it will get caught up somewhere and turkey vultures will eat it. It's too bad your sons won't get to know where you are or if someone killed you," he chuckled.

At the mention of her sons, Maggie felt a surge of fury and strength as she sprung up, dizzy with pain, and faced him. She grabbed the hidden gun on her waistband and fired.

One shot hit the bomber in his shoulder. There was a look of shock on his face that suddenly turned to a look of pure animal hatred as he gritted his teeth. He looked like a wild animal as he aimed his gun at her.

"Enough play. Now you die," he hissed at her.

Maggie had her gun still pointed at him, but just then a shot rang out. Maggie dove for the ground. The killer had a surprised look on his face as he stumbled back and fell into the darkness off the cliff.

Chapter 37

Maggie kept totally still until she suddenly heard Mike's voice.

"Maggie, it's okay. I got him. We got him." Mike rushed over to Maggie and gently said, "I want to see how badly hurt you are. I called for backup before I got here, and the medics are here now for you and the others. I want you to just lie here for a while before I move you."

Relief washed over Maggie. "Is Reggie okay?"

"She's hurt and needs to go to the hospital, but she's the one that pointed to where you were. She had her cell phone in her pocket and, believe it or not, when she heard my car pull up called me for help."

"What about Sam and Mrs. Stanley?"

Mike hesitated, tears welling in his eyes, "He got her… she's dead."

Maggie touched his cheek and said, "Oh no."

Mike said, "Reggie and Sam will survive, but they need

surgery. Sam was far enough from the cabin that he did not get burnt. But I am so sorry Mrs. Stanley didn't make it," Mike said sadly.

Mike then gently checked Maggie to see if she was okay and, feeling somewhat certain she did not have any neck or back injuries, helped her slowly up the hill. At the top of the hill another ambulance had arrived and a police car's lights spun.

In the light of the yard, Mike turned to Maggie as he held both of her hands in front of them. "You need to go over to the paramedics and have them take a look at you. He did a number on you, but you're alive, thank God," Mike said. "It was almost as if someone was guiding me to you tonight, besides Reggie. I just knew I could not lose you...I just couldn't."

Maggie felt a rush of emotion at his words and said, "I don't want to lose you either, Mike." And, in the quiet of her mind, Maggie thought, *Thank you, Henry, for bringing him to me*.

The EMTs tried to check Maggie, but she brushed them off. She needed to know how Reggie and Sam were doing. Sam had already left in one ambulance and Reggie was waiting in the second one when Maggie got into the back of the ambulance with help. When Reggie saw Maggie her tired eyes lit up. "I knew you wouldn't leave me. Boy, are you beat up," Reggie said weakly, grabbing for Maggie's hand, and they held on to each other for a moment.

Maggie said, "What is it with me getting hurt all the time? Go figure."

Reggie laughed, and then got very serious. "Did you get him?" Reggie said.

"He's dead. Mike shot him and he went over the cliff."

Mike came over. "Reggie, it's time to get to the hospital.

Our killer is dead. Our guys found his body and you don't have to worry. You ladies sure gave him a run for his money, and no doubt, Maggie, even if I hadn't shot him you probably would have sent him over that cliff."

Maggie said, "That may be true, because nobody is going to say they are going to hurt my kids or my family. But thank God you were there. I'd like to ride with Reggie to the hospital. I think we should call her parents, and I want to call my sons and tell them all is okay. They are going to be pissed off that I did not tell them more, but they're safe. I can't wait to talk to them."

Maggie looked at the shell of the cabin burnt to a crisp and felt sad for Mike.

"No matter what, I'm here for you, Maggie. You go with Reggie and I'll follow in my car."

"What about your cabin, Mike?"

"As long as you're safe, that's all that matters. A cabin is just a cabin." Mike gave Maggie a long hug, stepped out of the ambulance, and strode to his car. Maggie watched him as he stood by his car, and gave one last wave before he got in to follow the ambulance to the hospital.

EPILOGUE:

The party in Maggie's house was well attended. A few of the guests had stitches, Band-Aids, and gauzes, but thank God they were all alive. It had been a close call with Sam, but he had survived the brutal shooting. The story had been on the news many times, with Reggie being interviewed herself as one of those involved.

Maggie walked out on the deck where Mike, Reggie, Sam, Alice and her husband, and Maggie's two sons were all talking and laughing. She felt happy to see so many people she cared about in one place.

"I still can't believe that our guy was Tim." Sam said. "This guy used to come in the station all the time. It freaks me out that a normal looking guy who was so friendly to us, and who we had no idea was anything but a nice guy, was a vicious killer."

"I can't believe I never met this guy before," Mike said, bewildered. "Sure I probably saw him around town, but never

TOO LATE TO RUN

at the station."

"He even has a wife and friends, Mike. We checked out his house, his computer, and have spent hours interviewing his wife, but she was totally unaware that her husband did this. She thought we got the wrong guy, and boy, was she hysterical. When we proved it to her, revealing some of the things we found in a storage unit he'd rented, she was in shock. She left town to go to her parents' house, and who knows if she'll come back. We found lots of old pictures of Tim's dad and family, but there are no siblings, no aunt or uncles, and his dad and grandmother died in a car accident a number of years ago. What was strange was that in the storage locker we found boxes of bomb equipment. Not the sophisticated stuff he used, but old stuff."

"It still amazes me that he was the married guy my neighbor, Carol, was having an affair with. When she said what goes around comes around, little did she know she would give his name to all of you and also get the reward. She's lucky she wasn't killed." Reggie said.

As she said that, Reggie saw Mike's face change from laughter to sadness, and she said, "I am so sorry about Mrs. Stanley. I am glad you arranged the funeral and many of her friends attended."

"I may never forgive myself for involving her in this," Mike said. "But I will never forget her." They were all silent for a minute on the porch, and then Allen spoke up.

"What about the animal smuggling?" Allen asked.

"The raid went great, and the Fish and Wildlife Bureau along with the FBI made a big dent in the operation. They'll never shut it down totally, but it made a dent. With our bomber and the CEO of the Internet company both dead, this has shut it down in this town for sure," Mike said, as he pulled Maggie close to him and put his arm around her shoulder.

Maggie's sons had taken an instant liking to Mike, and even though it had been three weeks since the killer's death, she had made up for all her secrets by telling them everything, and talking to them more than she ever had before.

Maggie was bruised and battered, but she had survived, and she *was* going to be happy. Reggie and Sam were closer now, and Mike was becoming part of her daily life. He was still sad his cabin had burned down, but he said it would give him a project to build another in its place, and maybe Maggie could give him some decorating suggestions. She and Reggie talked all the time, and Reggie teased her on how the two of them should go after more bad guys. Mike had rolled his eyes and said, "Not without my backup."

As Maggie looked around at her loved ones, she smiled. How lucky she was, and who would have ever thought one day could change her entire life?

About the Author

Judy Snider lives in Virginia Beach, Virginia with her husband and two cats. She is the mother of two grown sons and has written award winning picture books, one co-authored by her sister. Judy is a retired social worker, a song lyricist and a community volunteer. She is excited to enter the world of writing suspense books with her first suspense novel. She is working on her second suspense novella which has a few of the characters from this book in it, and keeps the reader turning pages to see what will happen next.

To learn more about Judy go to www.judysnider.com

www.ingramcontent.com/pod-product-compliance
Lightning Source LLC
Chambersburg PA
CBHW022115170626
46808CB00002B/732